Trick-or [illegible] and More Twisted Dog Tales

AMY KRISTOFF

Deer Run Press
Cushing, Maine

Library of Congress Card Number: 2019933819

ISBN: 978-1-937869-09-0

First Printing, 2019

Published by
Deer Run Press
8 Cushing Road
Cushing, ME 04563

Contents

Trick-or-Treat

"Here come the Shiller girls," Cora said and closed the shutter slats of the living room window. What should she care if they saw her? Because she figured they were brats and would point and laugh at her.

The only element that indicated they had some sensibility was the fact the younger (and prettier) one, Gemma, was walking the family dog. He was a Mastiff named "Boris," and he was panting, although the three of them were walking quite slowly. It was very warm out even though it was barely 11:00 a.m. The weather here in Scottsdale, Arizona was pretty close to perfect by now, the day before Halloween.

The Shiller girls should have considered themselves too old to trick-or-treat, but they'd most likely be making the rounds in the name of showing off their elaborate costumes and getting free candy too. Their mother, Yvette, was probably behind it, at least the part about them showing off. The family lived in a sprawling, Mediterranean-style house halfway up the east side of Mummy Mountain but on the same street as Cora, Sandstone Place. The property was almost two acres but much of it was on the mountainside.

Cora's one-story, tan adobe-style house was on an acre and a half at the corner of Sandstone Place and Horseshoe Drive. The house itself was almost four-thousand square feet, which was more space than she needed. However, she wasn't going anywhere, having lived alone since her husband, Drew, passed away four years ago to the day! As far as being alone all that time, Cora still had her French bulldog, Spikey, until two years ago. She didn't acquire another canine companion because she seemed to prefer being alone. She spent a lot of time outside taking care of her property because she enjoyed doing so.

Regarding the Shiller family, the mother was a full-time socialite, whose goal in life appeared to be having her picture taken at as many charity functions as possible. Meanwhile Dad was constantly traveling, usually abroad. Whatever he did for a living was obviously very lucrative. His wife insisted upon an escort, so her husband must not have been the jealous type.

Cora couldn't figure out what bothered her about the Shiller girls, but they did, and she wanted to know why they weren't in school this morning. Maybe they went to public school and were on fall break. Was it possible the family was having money problems? Cora only asked that because she was pretty sure both girls had attended a private school on the East Coast. In fact she hadn't seen them in at least two and a half months, and suddenly they had been around this past week.

Both girls were so close in age, they could have been twins, at least from behind, as both were tall and lanky and had nearly-waist-length blond hair. As mentioned, however, the younger one, Gemma, was the prettier one. The truth of the matter was she looked like a more petite, younger version of her beautiful mother, while her sister, Cynthia, had a face like a bulldog. It was safe to say she'd inherited it from her father.

Seeing the Shiller sisters again walking the family dog had stirred something in Cora, making her wonder why she didn't finally get a French bulldog puppy. Despite how Cora might have sounded, she didn't feel sorry for herself. She'd had a wonderful marriage and she made sure to remember the great times Drew and she'd had. She also had a daughter and a preschool-age granddaughter, but they lived in San

Francisco. Nan, Cora's daughter, was still married to her daughter's father, but she was currently living with her "fiancé." Nan called Cora every other day, and she was sounding less and less enamored with the fiancé, whom she'd met at a restaurant—because he was her waiter! Not to put the man's profession down, but Nan had gone out with a couple girlfriends "to chill" (Nan's words), while her husband was at home watching their daughter, and she fell in love at first sight with the guy serving her drinks and dinner. Nan's sole justification for dumping her multi-millionaire, investment banker husband was she was "unhappy." Maybe her attitude was a product of the times, but Cora wanted to believe she'd raised a "better" daughter than that.

Cora just about had Nan convinced to come live with her for awhile. Naturally this invitation was extended so Cora could have her granddaughter with her. Admittedly Cora was skeptical of her daughter's attentiveness to her own child. Rather than be angry with Nan, why not take advantage of the situation? Truthfully Cora was at the point in her life it would be more fulfilling to have her granddaughter around the house than a puppy. That wasn't to say she didn't want a dog, but she'd wait to see what Nan decided to do.

As for the Shiller girls, Cora would have little time to concern herself about them if she was chasing after her granddaughter. Having a puppy would still allow her too much extra time. It wasn't healthy to be paranoid, whether or not you were justified in being so. What little Cora knew about the Shiller girls was from another neighbor who lived on Sandstone Place, namely Jean Plumb. She and her husband, Carson, owned an acre property with a two-story, brown adobe-style house, just shy of the gate at the end of the Shiller property, on the south side of Sandstone. The acre lot across the street was for sale, and Cora wondered why the Shillers didn't purchase it—foremost for "privacy." Secondly, wouldn't it be a good investment? Doug Shiller should have known all about that.

The other day Cora had seen the Shiller girls face-to-face, as she'd been in the front of her house, admiring how tall each saguaro cactus was on either side of the brown brick walkway leading to the rustic wood front door. Since she had a xeriscape "yard," raking and pulling errant weeds were Cora's principle tasks. A portion of the backyard had grass, although she was thinking of eliminating it if she didn't get another dog soon. She had a hand mower to keep it trim.

As the Shiller girls approached on the sidewalk, Cynthia walking Boris, her sister on her left, Cora waited to pull a couple weeds so she could first say hello to the two girls. They appeared almost shy when Cora greeted them, but once they'd passed her, both started laughing. It could have been over anything, but Cora could help taking their laughter "personally." That was when she decided her loneliness was having a negative effect on her.

Fortunately today the Shiller girls didn't notice Cora. Of course, she was inside and closed the shutter slats "in time," but something was "wrong" for Cora to be so ridiculously paranoid. It wasn't like she ever was before. As mentioned, it was no way to live.

Cora needed to call Jean Plumb and flat-out tell her the Shiller girls made her uneasy but couldn't figure out why. Did Jean have any ideas?

Fortunately Jean was home almost as much as Cora, so Cora got ahold of her right away. The two women exchanged greetings, and Cora began the conversation by asking her, "Did you buy much trick-or-treat candy for tomorrow night? Last year I bought two bags of Snickers® bars and only used half of one bag. And that was because of being very generous with who did show up."

Jean said, "I was thinking of leaving the lights off and sitting in the back of the house with just the television on and my two cats to keep me company. Carson is out of town until the end of the week. He took his yearly golf trip with three of his golf buddies. The only reason I don't get upset with him up and leaving for almost a whole week is he's in a good mood for a month or more afterward."

"Sandstone Place and Horseshoe Drive haven't had hardly any residents move away, so if any of the kids still trick-or-treat, they're pushing it as far as appropriateness," Cora remarked. She almost added something about her daughter not even wanting to trick-or-treat after fourth grade but held off. Jean had a grandson in fifth grade, and maybe he still trick-or-treated.

"Cynthia and Gemma Shiller will be trick-or-treating, I'd bet money on it," Jean remarked.

The back of Cora's neck felt prickly upon hearing those girls' names uttered. She asked Jean, "How old are they exactly?"

"Cynthia, the older one, is fourteen, and Gemma just turned twelve."

"I thought they were closer in age than that."

"Gemma's an intellectual genius," Jean said. "And that isn't a hollow boast from her mother. Gemma skipped a grade, so she's in a grade behind her sister."

"Oh, I see," Cora said, trying to fathom what went through a genius's mind when it came to assessing Cora Simms. After all, Gemma was the one who'd laughed the hardest when passing her house earlier. She added, "I have to admit, I find them both unsettling. I called you to see if you had any ideas why I'd feel this way. Both of them just passed my house walking their dog, Boris. I was outside last time and said hello, and they acknowledged me. Nonetheless, they laughed after passing by, and I can't get over the possibility they were laughing at me."

"They're just kids," Jean said. "Maybe they made some silly joke, but it's nothing to take personally. They're home from school for the rest of the week before they have to return for final exams."

"For the semester?"

"I believe so."

"After that they'll be back home until after the new year?"

"Probably," Jean answered. "They attend a private school in Virginia that has an equestrian program and they board their horses there."

"If that's the case, no wonder they're eager to walk the family dog," Cora remarked. "They're used to dealing with their big, luggy horses, but they're three-quarters of the country away. It must cost a fortune to ship them out there."

"They'll be shipped back here at the end of the school year, most likely. Their father, Doug, is the one who spends all kinds of money on the girls, and it just so happens his mother went to the same school they're attending. I wouldn't be surprised if Dottie was helping pay her grandkids' tuition, all in the hope they'll take to riding and showing like she did in her day."

"Does Yvette ride?" Cora wanted to know, trying to learn whatever she could about the Shillers. As it stood, there was nothing about Gemma and Cynthia that should have made Cora paranoid. At worst they were perhaps a bit spoiled.

"No, she doesn't have time. How could she when she's mugging for every camera shot at the latest philanthropic function? Moneybags Doug's the one who spoils them and since they go to an equestrian-themed boarding school, of course they each had to have a horse of her own. He'd contacted a trainer last spring and procured the horses through her. School time came around, and the horses were shipped off just like the kids. What a waste of money, if you ask me."

"I'm still digesting the fact they'll soon be home again to stay," Cora remarked, not intending to "think aloud." She could not figure out why the Shiller sisters were suddenly front and center in her life, in the physical sense, yet she hadn't noticed they'd been gone for two and half months, perhaps longer.

"I beg your pardon?" Jean asked.

"Nothing, Jean. I was absentmindedly talking out loud to myself. I guess that's what happens when you've been alone for awhile, as I've been."

"Cora, I worry about you," Jean said, sounding genuinely concerned. The two women had known one another since they and their respective husbands were simultaneously each having a house built across the street from one another (albeit not directly across). The Plumbs' property was much closer to the entryway of the Shillers'. The latter's house wasn't even completely visible from the street because it was about two-hundred feet away, via a very steep asphalt driveway. Yvette walked back and forth on the driveway a few times a day for a workout. She didn't go beyond the automatic gates because she didn't like to be seen in public! What utter hypocrisy.

Sometimes Jean Plumb felt sorry for Cora Simms, but it wasn't as if Cora's situation wasn't of her own making. She lost her husband a few years ago and her dog a couple years after that, but if she was so lonely, do something about it! Instead she appeared to wallow in her loneliness and sometimes made no secret of as much. Jean took it in stride until today, when Cora revealed a strange obsession with the Shiller girls. Undoubtedly Cora had no idea Jean was sufficiently perceptive to notice this. At the very least Cora needed to get a dog so she could have another living being with her. Otherwise she might go insane.

Cora had previously mentioned something about her daughter, Nan, and her granddaughter moving in with her, so perhaps she was waiting for them to arrive and get settled before adding a new puppy to the household. Cora was vague on the details as to why Nan was even considering moving to Scottsdale from California, so Jean was left to assume her marriage was in trouble. Not to judge Cora's abilities at child rearing, but she was awfully permissive raising Nan. Granted, she quit trick-or-treating after fourth grade, but that was because of her precociousness and had nothing to do with Cora telling her to quit. If anything, Cora always appeared to be afraid of her daughter. At the very least, Cora was concerned about aggravating her in any way, so she got what she deserved, not that Jean took any pride in stating as much about a friend and neighbor. It would certainly be interesting to see what happened if/when Nan Simms came home. Nan's last name was most likely something else, although she most likely was no longer sleeping with her husband. Not to be funny, but maybe things would be different with Nan today if she'd wanted to trick-or-treat a few more years. Jean was all for her grandson, James, being allowed to trick-or-treat as long as he wanted. (He was in fifth grade.) Therefore, despite her apparent criticism of the Shiller girls still trick-or-treating at ages 12 and 14, Jean was all for it. She only acted like she was critical of them to appease Cora.

Gemma and Cynthia were actually Jean's grand nieces, as their mother, Yvette, was Jean's sister's daughter. This was not something Cora Simms was even remotely aware of, but it wasn't as if Jean kept the familial tie a secret per se. It more or less came down to the fact her sister Julia's daughter Yvette was "technically" illegitimate, so Jean and Julia's mother refused to recognize Yvette as part of the family. Over time Yvette figured out what was going on and was all the more determined to "make something of herself." And she was probably in therapy. She kind of did "make it," marrying into major money. Stating as much was not in any way a testament to Jean's jealousy of her niece. Fortunately Yvette had enough class to keep a respectful distance and let Jean decide if they could have a relationship. When Yvette moved into the neighborhood a decade ago, it took Jean a couple years to even believe her illegitimate niece and her family were actually neighbors! Not only that, they lived in the most spectacular property on the street, not only because of the house itself but its location with panoramic views.

Meanwhile, Jean's husband, Carson, couldn't fathom why Jean didn't "make friends" with her niece. Jean had told him innumerable times, "It's too long of a story to explain. I'll wait until we have more time." They'd been married close to forty years, so it was safe to say they were running out of time.

Since it was the anniversary of Drew's passing, Cora typically marked the day by visiting him at the cemetery. The entire first year following his death, she went there daily, spending half an hour or longer at his gravesite, sobbing. On the one year anniversary of his passing, Cora visited him at the cemetery, but she didn't stand there and cry. Not only that, she felt pretty good, and she had an epiphany in which she realized it was time to celebrate Drew as he was, not grieve his death anymore. So she'd left the cemetery and went to lunch at "Rio's," one of their favorite restaurants, especially for lunch. They didn't go out at lunchtime until Drew's retirement, which he enjoyed for barely a year before passing away following complications from a heart attack.

That "first lunch alone at Rio's" was so enjoyable, Cora still remembered what she had: roast turkey on a sourdough bun with cranberry glaze and three kinds of melted cheese. She thought about that meal whenever she needed a pick-me-up, which seemed to be often. Not only that the outing created a precedent for every anniversary after that. She would visit Drew's gravesite and then go out to lunch, usually at Rio's. However, last year the food wasn't as good as it formerly was, so it was time to try a different place. Or maybe she needed to do something besides go out to lunch after visiting the cemetery.

Indeed, Cora nixed going out to lunch and decided to take a stroll through Fiesta Mall in Mesa. She made a point of going in "Pet's Paradise," aware the store offered puppies for sale. There was probably no chance a French bulldog puppy was part of their puppy inventory, so she was safe from making eye contact with one and having to bring him (or her) home. Although she had never purchased a dog from a pet shop, she was aware it was possible to "feel sorry" and make a purchase.

Only after Cora had walked through half of the lower level of the mall did she reach Pet's Paradise. The second she stepped inside the store and saw the two dozen glass cages on her right, stacked on two levels, she wondered what kind of "paradise" this was for the dogs housed in there. Thinking like that was Cora's first mistake. Then she made eye contact with a cute-as-a-button, female French bulldog puppy. The price was $950.00—"On Sale." Talk about preying on a customer's emotions.

Cora and the puppy spent a few minutes together in a play area, and she was compelled to purchase the dog. However, when the Pet's Paradise employee checked on Cora and the puppy, Cora said she was done and let the young woman put the puppy back in the cage. However, Cora stood in front of the cage and stared at the puppy after the employee left. She couldn't figure out if she was compelled to buy the dog to "save her" (the dog) or save herself—or both? Unable to arrive at an answer it seemed logical to leave, yet she couldn't get herself to move.

A girl of seven or eight waltzed in, her mother a few feet behind her, not moving as quickly because she was simultaneously texting on her phone. Cora pretended to be looking at all the puppies so the girl wouldn't make a point of looking at the French bulldog too.

Unfortunately the second the girl reached the French bulldog puppy's cage, she abruptly halted and declared, "Mom, that's the dog I want."

"Mom" managed to ignore her phone for a few seconds and put her nose against the glass as if she was inspecting the dog. Immediately Cora became possessive of the puppy and wanted the girl and her mother to leave as soon as possible. Admittedly the puppy didn't appear to mind the attention. Cora moved away from all the cages and pretended to be picking out a collar and leash on a rack facing the cages, hoping to eavesdrop on the mother-daughter conversation.

The two had a brief exchange Cora couldn't decipher and then the daughter asked, "Couldn't I at least play with the bulldog puppy for a minute?"

"No! We're just looking. I told you I'd only come in here if you promised not to complain about anything."

"I'm not complaining, Mom. I just wanted to see that one puppy for a minute."

"Fine," Mom said. "Just don't tell Dad tonight I let you look at a puppy because you might be able to get it. He'll kill me."

That did it, Cora was leaving. With Cora's luck the girl would be buying the French bulldog puppy, despite the mother's apparent hesitation to make any sort of commitment. The girl would get her way, just like Cora's daughter always did, especially if the girl was an only child, like Nan was.

Nan Simms was unofficially going by her maiden name because she couldn't stand the name she'd taken when marrying her #&*@ husband. No one could begin to understand how difficult it was to remain with a man who had 100% credibility on his side because of his money, status, power, etc. Meanwhile, she was anything but the ungrateful bitch who was looking for a huge payday when she divorced Rick. All she wanted at this point was some peace of mind. Speaking of, she must have temporarily lost it when she'd mistakenly thought she'd fallen in love with a man besides her husband. If anything she once loved Rick but no longer did because privately he had become a jerk. There were some shake-ups at his job, but was that sufficient reason to take it out on his wife? Maybe in regard to his line of work it was excusable, what did Nan know? She'd married when she was too young and naive. Then she got talked into having a kid, which wasn't fair. Therefore, Nan was going home to live with her mother because she made no secret of wanting to take care of her granddaughter. At the same time her mother pretended to be aloof about having her daughter and granddaughter come live with her. Nan had no intention of bothering to look for a job. It was too much work!

Driving home from the mall, Cora was in tears thinking about leaving the French bulldog puppy behind. She couldn't help herself, and she was aware her emotional outburst was aided by the fact it was the fourth anniversary of Drew's passing. Stopped at an intersection, Cora wiped her eyes with a tissue and thought about her visit to Pet's Paradise and wondered why "the girl" wasn't in school. Perhaps her mother home-schooled her, or she was on fall break. The most important question was: Why was Cora so affected by someone else wanting the French bulldog puppy? Obviously Cora had an opportunity to buy the dog herself!

Cora's stomach loudly growled, a reminder she'd forgotten to have lunch. Once the light changed she'd head to a fast-food restaurant drive-through. Also she still needed to pick up a bag of trick-or-treat candy.

Finally home, barely was Cora in the door when the phone started ringing. Time and again Nan had griped Cora needed a cell phone because she was "a pain to get ahold of, thanks to only having a landline." It wasn't like Cora went out much anyway, although she did spend a lot of time outside when she was home.

The caller was none other than Nan. Cora barely said hello before her daughter exclaimed, "I'll be there in the morning with Lily, Mom. I just booked my flight and I already have my stuff being put in storage. I can't take the drama here. Rick's threatening to permanently take Lily away from me, and neither one of us has even filed for divorce. My fiancé is most definitely an ex, so I'm no longer welcome at his place. He never liked Lily anyway, so that part of my personal soap opera worked itself out. The one credit card of my own will be up to its limit by the time I leave the hotel tomorrow, so I'll be arriving completely broke!"

Cora had felt her stomach tighten more and more as her daughter spoke. At this point she wasn't even hungry. She wanted nothing more than to scream, "Nanette, can't you at least try to work things out with either your husband or your fiancé before running away?" However, she didn't say anything. Not only that, she didn't question whether her daughter was even telling the truth.

Nan offered to take a cab from the airport, using the last bit of cash she had to her name. Cora didn't say a word to deter her from that plan, which possibly upset her daughter. Good. It was about time she learned what it felt like to expect something and not get it.

Despite knowing she had but one "free evening" before her peace and quiet would be erased, Cora couldn't relax and enjoy it because in a few hours she had to wait for the trick-or-treaters.

Not one trick-or-treater came to Cora's house. She couldn't believe it. Not even the Shiller girls made an appearance! Did they purposely not come to her house, or did they finally realize they were getting too old to trick-or-treat? Maybe their mother was in agreement.

It bothered the heck out of Cora, the Shiller girls were no-shows. To think, she should have been relieved! The truth of the matter was they bothered her more when they were nowhere to be seen.

That thought and the fact no one else showed up exhausted Cora, and she couldn't wait to go to bed. Besides, she needed plenty of rest before Nan and Lily's arrival tomorrow.

Although Cora occasionally had insomnia, she usually managed to get through it by doing some reading. However, that didn't appear to work on the very night it was imperative she get plenty of sleep. The problem was she kept thinking about the French bulldog puppy, how she'd callously left her in that hideous glass cage.

The only way Cora could finally relax was by promising herself she'd be at Pet's Paradise as soon as it opened in the morning, to purchase the French bulldog puppy. Finally Cora fell asleep.

The following morning Cora arrived a little early at Fiesta Mall, and although she was able to enter the mall itself, none of the stores were yet open. She patiently waited outside Pet's Paradise, along with a couple other customers. The entire time all she could think about was the possibility they too were here to purchase the French bulldog puppy. The mere thought made her extremely anxious.

After seemingly more than just a few minutes, Pet's Paradise was finally open. Naturally Cora went straight to the French bulldog puppy's cage, figuring everyone was headed there. The good news was no one else did, but the bad news was the puppy was no longer in her cage. Not only that, a "Sold" sign was on the front of it! A couple other puppies were looking at her, but she couldn't focus on anything other than the empty cage where the French bulldog puppy had been. Describing Cora as devastated would have been an understatement.

Before anyone could ask her if she needed any help, Cora departed the store. Back home, she couldn't pull into the driveway of her house because who was passing by on the sidewalk but the Shiller sisters. Cynthia was walking Boris, and Gemma was carrying a puppy. The animal was easier to discern because her red leash was trailing down the side of Gemma's bare leg. (She was wearing especially short denim shorts this morning.)

As Cora waited for the sisters to pass by, she got another look at the puppy and determined it was none other than the French bulldog puppy from Pet's Paradise. It was possible they in fact didn't trick-or-treat at all last evening because their mother took them to the mall to buy the puppy. Didn't that scenario just figure? At least the puppy was in good hands, for the most part. She would never be overweight, given how the Shiller girls liked to walk Boris.

Cora's plan for the remainder of the day until Nan and Lily showed up was to straighten the house up and get two bedrooms ready. The house had four bedrooms in all, including the master bedroom. However, Drew had turned one of them into an office for his mediation practice. It was still his office in a way, given how many of his papers remained in the same place he'd left them. Even a pair of his reading glasses was still sitting on a shelf. If Cora absolutely had to use the computer she did so but preferred to stay out of the room. It was inevitable Nan would want to use the computer, so Cora was already anticipating getting a lecture on how she hadn't kept it updated, etc. Cora was willing to take her daughter's criticisms in stride, but Nan had better be prepared to be criticized a little, too. As it was, Cora was aware of what she'd helped create in her daughter, but it was never too late to try and change her—was it?

About 2:30 Nan called from the airport in San Francisco. Her flight was delayed boarding for some inexplicable reason. Lily was getting irate and unmanageable. Nan was going to wait "an hour, tops," before she was going to think of another plan. A couple girlfriends had generously offered a spare bedroom Lily and she could share for several nights if need be. Cora was aware she should have been relieved it was possible Nan would be staying put, but she inevitably thought of Lily and her heart ached for her granddaughter. Nan was supposed to have enrolled her in nursery school but couldn't seem to stay in one place long enough.

Looking out the living room window following the phone call, Cora saw none other than the French bulldog puppy walking on the sidewalk, not even a leash dragging behind her. Neither was there a sign of the Shiller sisters, nor Boris. Therefore, Cora bolted outside to better see what exactly was going on. Fortunately Sandstone Place wasn't a busy street, so there was little danger of the puppy getting hit by a vehicle if she went in the street. Cora was hurrying out the door because she felt like the puppy was "there for the taking." Clearly she was very much thinking in the moment.

Once upon the puppy Cora couldn't wait to scoop her up, and it seemed as if the puppy was relieved to be rescued. Cora couldn't take her in the house fast enough, wanting to cherish a few minutes with the puppy before it was necessary she alert the rightful owners of their puppy's whereabouts.

Cora ended up taking the puppy to the backyard, where she finally set her down. Then she went in search of her beloved Spikey's water bowl. After his passing Cora had saved most of his belongings, as she couldn't bear to throw hardly anything out, just like with Drew's possessions.

The puppy drank almost the whole bowl of water. Although it wasn't a large bowl, the puppy was pretty small. It made Cora wonder about the circumstances surrounding why the puppy was loose to begin with. Maybe she was left outside with Boris (who drank all the water in their shared bowl), and she was afraid of him so she managed to escape. As it was, possibly Boris was a lot meaner when no people were around and enjoyed intimidating the puppy.

After spending a few minutes petting the puppy, Cora started to feel guilty because of failing to contact the Shillers. Ideally she needed to return the animal. However, there was a problem: although they lived a few hundred yards away, she wasn't about to scale the austere-looking gate at the entrance to their property, French bulldog puppy in tow. The Shillers weren't listed in the phone book, so Cora's only hope was to contact a member of the family via cell phone—except she didn't know anyone's number. Jean Plumb seemed to know them pretty well, so the best thing to do was call her and tell her the situation. At the very least maybe she could relay the message via social media, as she was more into modern technology than Cora.

Jean answered the phone right away, and Cora filled her

in on everything involving the Shillers relative to the French bulldog puppy (or what she assumed to be the actual circumstances). Jean told Cora she'd call Yvette and let her know what was going on and then call Cora back.

A couple minutes later Jean did so and told Cora Yvette didn't answer. Most likely she was taking the kids to the airport, as they had to return to school for their semester exams. She advised Cora to call the father's business number and let him know what was going on.

Cora couldn't fathom why Jean gave her that number but didn't give her Yvette's cell phone number, which Cora would have preferred calling. Why bother the family breadwinner at his place of business over a runaway dog? It almost seemed like Jean was doing this to Cora on purpose.

Before calling Mr. Shiller, Cora spent a few more minutes petting the puppy and talking to her. When she finally called "Shiller Incorporated, LLC," a secretary named Brenda answered. When asked if Mr. Shiller was available, she didn't even ask for Cora's name or her reason for calling. Instead she forwarded the call to Mr. Shiller, who identified himself as "Doug" and asked, "How can I help you?"

Cora proceeded to identify herself as well and explained the dilemma involving the French bulldog puppy, how she saw one of his daughters with the puppy, and later it was seen walking around loose in front of her house. She left out the fact she had passed on the puppy when she was at Pet's Paradise (but wanted her).

Mr. Shiller confessed to not being up on the daily happenings at home, as he had been out of the country for "several weeks." Cora took that to mean he was skeptical and suspected she could be making up the entire story. As pleasant-sounding as he was, it was plain he had no interest in dealing with an issue involving a runaway pet shop puppy his wife and daughters supposedly recently purchased. He gave Cora Yvette's cell phone number and said, "She's really the one to talk to. If she doesn't answer, just leave a message.

Thank you. Good-bye."

The last thing Cora was in a hurry to do was call Yvette Shiller. It was more gratifying to pet the puppy for a few more minutes. She told the puppy, "Too much longer with us being together and I'll have to name you," knowing it was "dangerous" to talk like that or she'd never call Yvette Shiller.

But Cora finally did call her. Just like with Jean, there was no answer, and Cora considered leaving a message. However, she decided to call back in a few minutes and leave a message then if Yvette still didn't answer. In the meantime she'd indulge in petting the puppy for a few more minutes.

Cora was thirsty, so she went in the house to get an iced tea, leaving the puppy on the patio. Even though she was free to roam around the walled backyard, she appeared to be the happiest sitting on the Saltillo tile, near the black wrought-iron chaise longue on which Cora had been sitting.

The phone rang. Before answering Cora glanced at her watch and realized it had already been an hour since Nan called. Not even looking at the caller I.D. for her landline phone, Cora was certain the caller was her daughter. It helped Cora anticipated as much because the second she picked up the receiver Nan announced, "Mom, I'm in line to board, finally. I was about to lose my mind and give up waiting. I'll call you again after landing so you have an idea when I'll be there."

"Thanks," Cora said but Nan had already ended the call.

This was the beginning of the rest of Nan's life, and she was in a celebratory mood. She wanted a drink but her kid was with her, and she was frankly very paranoid about "being watched," even on an airplane! Nan's soon-to-be (hopefully) ex-husband had the financial means to hire a private investigator to follow her everywhere if need be. His sole purpose would be to catch her not being a perfect mother and she would lose sole custody of Lily in the divorce settlement. He undoubtedly "ran the numbers" and figured out he'd be money ahead if he paid the private investigator, and once Rick (her husband) had his "proof," Nan wouldn't get a dime for child support. She was counting on that to pad her wallet so she'd never have to work—despite what her mother was most likely counting on. If her mother hadn't figured out by now her daughter was a lazy b— she never would! It couldn't be emphasized enough, however, Nan wasn't divorcing for the money. Since her insolent husband had become such an ass, she might as well get as much out of him as she could.

What really got Nan pissed off was the fact Rick wanted a kid in the worst way, so she gave him one and he didn't care about either one of them. It was like Nan turned into a three-headed monster in his eyes after she gave birth. Lily might as well have been her three-headed offspring. Naturally Rick would argue she wasn't understanding about his stress because of his job, but it was difficult to be on the receiving end.

On the short flight from San Francisco to Phoenix it would be a lot to ask for Nan to meet a rich businessman (preferably never married but divorced would have to do). It was no help, having her daughter along. However, it was important to remain optimistic. Her daughter in the crowded middle seat, managed to fall asleep. Maybe she'd have a drink after all. It would take the last few dollars she had on her, but she was seriously needing a stress-reliever. Just the thought of "moving back home" upset her. Her mother could be so regimental. It would be comical if Nan wasn't forced to live it—the second time around!

Nan got her drink, took a couple welcomed sips and then happened to look at the guy in the window seat, to the right of her sleeping daughter, and he was purposely making bodily contact with her, moving his left arm just so. In that moment something awakened in Nan to make her a fiercely protective mother, so she proceeded to throw the remainder of the drink at the guy's face. His eyes weren't closed but were downcast, so at least the alcohol didn't go directly in them.

The event could have gone "unnoticed" if the pervert had taken the dousing like a man. Lily got a few drops on her and she didn't even wake up. She did, however, when the guy yelled, "What the # *& # you #@&*!" That of course brought a flight attendant as well as an air marshal.

Although Nan was aware this was no time for humor, her first thought nonetheless was about her ride to her mother's. It wouldn't cost her anything not because Mom would pick her up but a cop would be driving her there—once she told her story and "cleared her name." That was what she was planning to do, anyway. As it was, this situation would probably cause her to lose custody of Lily for sure, as the argument would be made she couldn't control herself. The irony was Nan finally felt like "a real mother."

Cora about fainted when the caller I.D. on the phone in her kitchen indicated it was the Phoenix Police Department. Immediately she feared she was being contacted because of her having taken in the Shillers' new French bulldog puppy.

Quickly Cora put together an excuse as to why she hadn't yet returned the puppy to her rightful owners before answering the phone and hearing: "Mrs. Simms? I have your daughter, Ms. Nanette Simms-Faus with me and her daughter Lily." Cora had to grab the corner of the kitchen countertop after listening to that introduction.

"What happened?" Cora asked, hardly able to believe she was having to pose this question to an officer of the law. She was starting to feel faint again.

"Nothing of terrific consequence, as it turned out," the man said. "She was able to recount the unfolding of events sufficiently so there was no reason to pursue any sort of investigation and the actual perpetrator of misconduct was let go because of a lack of eyewitness accounts, other than that of your daughter's. Both she and her daughter are here at the station, so I called a taxi driver bring them to your house, as I understand they are in town to stay for awhile?"

"Yes, that is correct," Cora replied. She wanted to be as succinct as possible because she felt like she was teetering on the edge of doing something terribly wrong. She of all people! Obviously Nan had just been teetering on that very same edge, and Cora didn't want to put her in "renewed jeopardy" of arrest.

Barely did Lily come in the house ahead of her mother, and she managed to see the French bulldog puppy—who was still on the patio. The double glass doors leading to the patio were both open, and the puppy proceeded to tear through the house to greet Lily, as if the two were lifelong friends.

Cora nearly cried, witnessing the two interact. Meanwhile, the taxi driver appeared with a couple large suitcases and set them in the white-tiled foyer. Nan looked in her wallet and exclaimed, "I don't have any money left!" and then winked at the guy. Cora missed the brief interaction because she was already running to get her purse, saying, "I'll take care of it, Nan." She was so happy to have her granddaughter here, nothing else mattered. She'd call Yvette Shiller's number again in a few minutes. This moment was so enjoyable Cora never wanted it to end. The puppy had made Lily's day—and Cora's, too.

"Don't I know you?" Yvette Shiller asked a gorgeous woman who was standing in the entryway of "Fran's," a new restaurant that had more business than available tables—and no reservations accepted. One more look at the woman and Yvette realized she did indeed know her; she was Nan Simms, a former neighbor. The man with her was very tall and handsome, and he couldn't seem to take his eyes off Nan. Last Yvette heard, Nan was married, and this guy did not appear to be her husband.

Finally Nan turned and acknowledged Yvette, saying, "I'm Nan Simms. Until I became Nan Simms-Faus. I think I may know you for sure."

Yvette introduced herself and Nan said, "I thought so!" Meanwhile the latter's "date" looked on approvingly. As for Yvette's "date," he appeared eager to either get a table or get out of the "cozy" restaurant.

There was a short wait until either couple could be seated, which wasn't bad, considering how crazy this place got on the weekends. Fortunately it was open for dinner seven nights a week, or the restaurant would be flooded with patrons all the hours it was open. Yvette felt an obligation to make conversation with Nan, simply because Yvette was so sociable (or so she liked to think). She didn't care if her escort wanted Yvette to keep to herself so as not to draw attention. Since Yvette's husband knew she had male companionship whenever she pleased, it didn't matter what the public chose to assume. It wasn't like she was having an affair. Remaining married was too financially rewarding to throw everything away.

Anyway, Yvette could not think of anything to say to Nan, but Nan saved the day by asking, "Did you see the puppy my mother just got? My daughter has already fallen in love with it. We may never be able to return to California because of the puppy."

Yvette wanted to know, "What kind of dog is it?"

"What kind?"

"Yes. Like what breed?"

"Oh. I'm not sure," Nan replied. "My mom had a French bulldog before, so that's probably what this one is. Mom's not one for change."

Yvette didn't say a word. She had known better than to leave the housekeeper, Mattie, home alone with Boris and "the new dog," who hadn't even been named yet. Yvette had gone with her daughters to Fiesta Mall to clothes shop before they went back to school, as neither one wanted to trick-or-treat. The three of them stopped in the pet shop and walked back out with a female French bulldog puppy. Mattie had made no secret of detesting the puppy upon first sight. Late the next morning, Yvette took Cynthia and Gemma to the airport so they could return to school in Virginia. Afterward, Yvette had gone shopping with a couple girlfriends and wasn't home the rest of the day, forgetting her cell phone.

Yvette and her escort's table was ready, so she was immediately whisked away to the dining room. Before leaving Nan, however, Yvette told her, "Tell your mother I said 'hello' and best of luck to her and her new puppy."

The Good Wife

Head in her hands, this was no way to be sitting at the kitchen table, where Alana was supposed to be having breakfast. She'd toasted two slices of homemade cinnamon raisin bread and slathered them with margarine. Also on the table was a steaming-hot mug of strong, black coffee. If it got even lukewarm she didn't want it, so she needed to get going and at least drink the coffee.

Instead Alana got up and stared out the window above the kitchen sink. Since it overlooked the carport attached to the house (which was her husband's idea, while she wanted a free-standing carport), there wasn't much to see, other than her red Nissan Sentra and Chris' white Chevrolet Colorado, which she was thinking about keeping since it was paid for. Grieving was a lousy reason to take off a few pounds, but she might do so because of how hard she was taking the sudden loss of her husband, two weeks ago. He'd collapsed and died in the kitchen after feeding the dogs lunch. It already seemed like years since he passed away. Maybe it had to do with the fact Chris and she been married for close to two decades. That was a long time, given some of the differences they had. Luckily Alana never raised suspicions about having a dark side, something not even she was aware of.

Having grown up in a "No Dog" household in Glendale, Arizona, Alana was desperate to own a dog by the time she graduated from high school. She only got passing grades so she could be certain to finish school at eighteen. That was her key to getting out from under her controlling, emotionally-abusive mother. It wasn't anything to complain about, Alana was the first to agree. However, everything convened to make her determined to find a way out, and her options were limited if she wasn't going away to college, or she did not yet have any job skills. Logically, getting married was her "out."

Fortuitously Alana's high school sweetheart, Chris, really did love her (he was mature beyond his years). Alana was pretty mature too, at least when it came to recognizing what she needed to do to get away from her ruinous life. Alana's father never divorced her mother, but he had hardly ever lived with either of them. It was strange, no two ways about it.

Anyway, Alana asked Chris to propose if he was serious about his love for her. Since he had already been attending a trade school while finishing high school, she knew he would be starting a new career not long after graduating. For a time they might have to live in the lower level of his parents' bi-level, but he had talked about wanting a place of his own since sophomore year. His drive and determination turned other girls off, but she'd always admired that about him. That made her a stand-out, and it came in handy when she needed a knight in shining armor to save her. (Chris was never really aware of how Alana felt about leaving home.)

Chris and Alana didn't have a "perfect life," but whose was? He was good-looking, hard-working, funny, polite, remembered her birthday, etc. Although for several years they'd wanted a family, Alana couldn't get pregnant. Chris was adamant they had a kid "the natural way or not at all." She didn't dare bring up adoption because that would have been even more out of the question than other options. Rather than despair, Alana would remind herself, her life was so much better than it was before! Meanwhile, her mother, Rachel, was more miserable than ever. Having her daughter leave home for good must have marked the beginning of the end for her.

Ten years in (the marriage), Alana still madly loved her husband, and he was equally in love with her. He seemed totally unconcerned no kids were in the picture, while Alana had resigned herself to the fact. His parents brought up the topic from time to time but overall appeared resigned as well, concerning the possibility their son and daughter-in-law were going to make them grandparents. Chris' sister, Kelly, was their only hope, and she was happier being an elementary school teacher and working with children than having a kid of her own. Her husband, Lou, was also a teacher (junior high school Spanish) and felt the same way.

During that same ten-year span of time, Alana became completely estranged from her mother. It was especially sad because her mother would need to be placed in assisted living soon—yet Alana didn't feel sorry for her. Come to find out from her mother's physician, for many years she had been addicted to painkillers she'd purchased online without a prescription. Suddenly it didn't seem so strange she was always crabby; she'd been living in a drug-induced haze!

Alana suddenly felt much better and sat back down at the kitchen table to eat the delicious breakfast she'd left untouched. Fortunately the coffee was still just warm enough to be drinkable. She polished off the two slices of cinnamon raisin toast in no time and got up to toast one more slice. Finally her appetite had returned. She didn't want to be too thin. Men didn't like dating women who looked like they wouldn't eat dinner if taken out to a "nice" (pricey) restaurant. After all, even though Alana was in the throes of grieving the loss of her husband, she had every intention of tying the knot again. She was only 38! And he'd have to like dogs. Talk about one of the differences Chris and she had. It never occurred to her a down-to-earth kind of guy wouldn't want a dog around the house. He didn't even want one that would have lived outside. That was a very unpleasant revelation, made after they were married. Alana probably would have married him anyway if she had found out beforehand.

Not only did Alana's mother end up in an assisted living facility at age forty-nine, she passed away barely two years after that. Alana couldn't even get herself to cry. Her father, Wright, showed up for the brief funeral service (everything was carried out per Alana's mother's wishes), hugged his daughter and said good-bye again, just like that. Having never tried to contact him because she'd feared "further estranging him," she vowed to keep up the same charade. She wasn't big on social media, other than keeping up with what her close circle of friends was up to. Her father was still married to Alana's mother when she passed away, so he got everything. Alana never questioned as much because she didn't want to appear greedy, although financial gain would have been the last thing on her mind.

As for Chris? He didn't even have a will, but Alana didn't have to worry because she "got everything" for a change. Neither had Chris made any burial arrangements, so there was no wake or funeral, which was what she wanted.

Going into the second decade of a blissful married life, Alana finally relaxed somewhat, but she stayed busy with a couple part-time jobs, both of them as a cashier. Still, she had plenty of time to think, and she decided it was time for Chris and her to own a dog. It wasn't like they didn't have the means, not to mention a perfect set-up: almost an acre behind their house in Chandler was enclosed by a concrete block wall. Also, a large mesquite tree in the middle provided plenty of shade. The dog could even retreat to the covered patio, where he could lie on the cool concrete.

Alana would take any dog at this point, and she intended to somehow miraculously change Chris' mind. He came home from work around 5:30. Since all of Alana's four-hour work shifts started in the morning and early afternoon, she was always home in time to serve him dinner. Alana liked to think she helped keep their marriage intact by making sure her husband enjoyed a home-cooked meal every night of the week.

What Alana would typically do was prepare the main course in the morning before leaving for work at her first job. While home between jobs one and two, she'd do some more preparation or set the timer on the oven and leave the main course in there. It would be ready when she returned home, usually half an hour before Chris.

Didn't her effort to make dinner year after year deserve a "reward"? Alana thought so. She'd "feed" Chris and then spring the request about getting a dog, on him. It just so happened she'd prepared his favorite meal: "stuffed meatloaf," a personalized version. Alana followed a recipe that required Swiss cheese and ham slices as the fillers, but Chris also wanted sliced boiled egg in there, too. He liked the meatloaf so much he never wanted any side dishes so he could "pig out on the meatloaf."

No matter what Alana served for dinner, she always set the table with steak knives, which happened to be a wedding gift from her mother. Funny she would bother to splurge on a gift. Anyway, Chris would complain he couldn't cut anything unless he had a steak knife. It used to be comical, how picky he could be about some things, but lately he was getting on her nerves. She still loved him, but at this point in their life together, she needed more breathing room.

At first Chris ate more voraciously than ever, which Alana found flattering. The more she watched him, however, she started to think his eating habits were disgusting. At the same time, she found it more pressing than ever to bring up the subject of acquiring a dog. Or more. She wanted enough dogs to make up for the fact she never had one at all.

Chris finally stopped stuffing his face long enough to take note of the fact his wife was staring at him, looking none too pleased. Rather than dig into a second thick slice of stuffed meatloaf, he asked her, "What's wrong?"

Alana was well-aware her husband only asked that when

he was really frustrated and truthfully didn't care what/if something was in fact wrong. If he couldn't figure out he ate like a slob, it was time she point it out. The thing was, why did it take her two decades to notice?

That question was of secondary importance because she was about to ask him the one that was foremost on her mind: "I've been thinking about getting a dog, and I'm hoping you'll agree it's a good idea. If you don't want us to spend much we could go to the shelter together and adopt a rescue."

Rather than offer any sort of response, Chris smiled and proceeded to serve himself another generous slice of stuffed meatloaf. Then he set to eating it like he didn't have a care in the world.

Alana "let" her husband eat for easily a minute before declaring, "We're going to the shelter tomorrow. You usually get off work early on Fridays, and the shelter closes at five-thirty. We can at least look at the dogs and go back Saturday and take care of the paperwork, if the dog we pick out is still available."

Chris must have been shocked by Alana's un-characteristically assertive behavior because he actually stopped eating long enough to nod and tell her, "O.K."

On Friday, Alana felt like she needed to hurry so she could be ready and waiting when Chris came home from work and they could leave right away for the closest shelter. It was on Saguaro Parkway, a quarter of a mile west of the 101 Freeway exit, on the right hand side of the road. The two-story facility was bright, clean and new, with adoptable kittens and cats on the second floor, puppies and dogs on the first. That was helpful because Alana knew Chris would be literally dragging his feet the whole way. She was frankly amazed she'd "told him" they were going to the shelter after he got off work. As it was, he never had anything else to do on a Friday afternoon, a long weekend looming ahead.

All this put another way? Chris had better come home

right after work. If he didn't, it would be unprecedented, and he'd have to be doing so on purpose. It was impossible he had "car trouble" because he was a mechanic!

Chris didn't come home at 4:00, as was agreed upon. Alana was particularly floored because she'd taken off early from her second part-time job and purposely gave no warning so she didn't use up her "non-emergency excuses." So she actually lied and pretended there was a crisis at home and she had to leave. Chris blew her off and a lot more would be at stake than them not getting a dog or two.

In the meantime Alana had plenty of time to finish the entrée she'd begun preparing. It was called "Spanish Chicken," a dish her mother often prepared. Her mother's faults aside, she was a pretty good cook. It was one meal Alana was guilty of gorging on, especially when she prepared it. (She liked to think she was a better cook than her mother, rest her soul.) As much as Alana was looking forward to dinner, she was more looking forward to the trip to the shelter. It was 4:30. She tried calling Chris' cell phone, no answer. She'd text him in a few minutes if he didn't come home. It was highly unlikely he got waylaid at work, but it was possible. He might have another, flimsy excuse, such as a co-worker had a pregnant wife or girlfriend, so there was a last-minute, after-work celebration.

Five o'clock. No Chris and he still wouldn't answer his phone. Not only that, Alana had texted him fifteen minutes ago and asked him (in all block letters), "WHERE ARE YOU?" He might as well have been on the moon.

Alana would wait. And wait some more, if need be. She really did still love her husband, but there truly was a thin line between love and hate. When he got home, she wouldn't press him for an answer as to why he was late but would still ask. And she would adopt as many dogs as she wanted.

"Honey, I have to confess, I never knew just how important it was for you to own a dog . . . or more," Chris told

Alana as they walked all four of their dogs (of various backgrounds, as each one was a rescue) on a Saturday morning, a couple months after they'd first visited a shelter.

"Now you do, Chris," Alana told him. "Another big one is how much I wanted to leave home right after I finished high school."

Chris almost stopped walking to ask his wife, "So you never really loved me?"

"Sure I . . . did," Alana replied, unable to resist "playfully" squeezing his arm, not the one holding the leashes for "Caramel" and "Candy," both stubby-legged with elongated bodies and oversized ears, indicating each one had some Corgi in her. However, Candy had a long tail, so she was probably the Cardigan Corgi of the two, unless that was thanks to the Beagle in her. Since Alana never previously had a dog, she "made do" by learning about many of the breeds. At the same time, she liked mixed-breed dogs just as much.

Alana was in charge of "Dori" and "Dani," two terrier mixes. Thankfully the four got along very well, which may or may not have been thanks to the fact they were all spayed. Alana had read conflicting articles regarding whether or not that figured into the dogs' attitudes toward one another.

Chris and Alana walked a hundred yards or more, neither one saying a word. For Alana's part, there was so much she wanted to say, it was impossible to know where to begin. Meanwhile, Chris' jaw was clenched, which was not a good sign, not that Alana particularly gave a s—t about his mental state at this point. The number one reason she'd married him, she'd come to realize, was her fear of being all alone. Her mother had brainwashed her into thinking no one would ever love her, and owning a dog was a waste of time. It was a good thing Alana never paid too much attention to her, past the emotional destruction.

Suddenly Alana asked, "I know I asked you this once already, but you wouldn't answer me previously and even said it was none of my business. Why were you late coming home that Friday we were supposed to go to the shelter?"

"Why are you bringing this up again? We miraculously acquired four dogs since then even though we didn't end up going there until the next day. What more could you want, Alana?"

"For you to answer the question, Chris."

"O.K. After we get home."

"I'm holding you to it."

"Fine with me."

Upon their return, Chris was insistent he feed the dogs lunch, even though it was a little early. He didn't even like that task and typically left it up to Alana if both of them were home.

Alana knew exactly what Chris was up to: attempting to avoid her, so he didn't have to finally answer her question from two months ago. How much longer did he think he could avoid his wife? Having "made her husband" go to the shelter (if only a day late), Alana felt she deserved to get her way with him, regarding everything. Or else.

As Chris fed the dogs in the utility room, Alana stood in the kitchen, still holding the leashes, too distracted to put them away. And it turned out she'd had a use for them, other than for taking the dogs on another walk. Anger gave her seemingly unlimited strength, which she was compelled to use.

Alana would feel better, she just needed to let time pass. Fortunately she still had her four adopted dogs. She just wished things didn't have to end the way they did. In other words, she didn't miss her husband but she did love him until she did some digging and realized he wasn't such a find after all, since he couldn't resist cheating on her with his boss' daughter, who answered the phone for "Big Bill's Auto Repair." She was pretty, how could Chris not notice that? Also she was very flirtatious. That was no excuse on Chris' part to cheat, but he figured once was O.K., especially since Alana had told him to do something.

Chris mentioned how angry he was that Friday he was supposed to go with Alana to the animal shelter, doing so the second he emerged from his truck. She was standing under the carport, between the house and her car. Chris got in her face and wagged a finger at her, declaring, "I came home when I wanted to. If you have a problem with it, tough shit."

Alana was so furious it took all she had not to find something to hurl at her husband's head, aiming at the middle of his forehead. She vowed to walk away and cool off, not look for something to use as a weapon. Before walking away, however, she asked him, "So why were you so late coming home?"

"None of your business!" he'd replied.

That response gave Alana all the verification she needed, her husband was no good.

He Never Really Was

Dee's mother, Jolene, once revealed she thought she was going to lose her daughter shortly after Dee came into the world. Jolene was hysterical and later swore her hyper-kinetic fit was what saved her newborn daughter's life. As Dee (Desiree) was being taken away, Jolene screamed so loudly and forcefully, she determined it was what jumpstarted her daughter's heart. Although a miracle had occurred, the hospital staff brushed the whole episode off as "coincidental." Jolene knew better.

That was Dee Horst's beginning, so it was no surprise she might come upon an incredible experience or two later in life. Indeed, one involved her fiancé, who'd just proposed to her. There was no ring, but Dee had told Sam, "Yes!" Of course she did because he'd suddenly reappeared after "disappearing" for a couple months. They had amicably agreed to break up at that point, but it was as if he had died. Since he could only be reached by a landline Dee was "forbidden" from calling, she respectfully didn't contact him. She'd just wanted to ask him how he was doing. She didn't even mind if he was seeing someone new. (Truthfully she kind of did, but she was happy being friends with her ex-boyfriend, if that was the best she could do.)

Although Dee hadn't received an engagement ring from Sam, he had presented her with a life-sized, stuffed Cocker Spaniel. He was aware she wanted a dog but worked such long hours, it wouldn't have been realistic to own one. Her dream was to save enough money so she could eventually quit her job at "South-West Web Hosting," based in Phoenix, and start her own web hosting business, working out of her house. Then she could have a dog or two, maybe even a couple horses, as her property was almost two acres, with a four-stall metal barn and a paddock, behind the house. Around her neighborhood about every other resident had a horse or two in the backyard, as it was very common to keep horses as pets. One neighbor even had a camel, which she took for a walk every day, right down Charter Oak Road.

Sam "came and went" the entire six months Dee and he "dated," if you could call it that. He still had his own place but wouldn't invite Dee there because it was "too messy." However, whenever he stayed with her, he was very fastidious. Dee found that very suspicious, as in he was lying about being single. She checked out what she could about him online, and it appeared he was telling the truth. However, his house was owned by his mother, which may have been why Dee wasn't welcome there. In other words, his mother, Susan, had a "no girlfriends" rule.

How Sam and Dee met was a bit "different," in and of itself. She was backing out of her driveway, in a hurry because she was yet again late to work. Admittedly she failed to look to her left as well as she should have, particularly when the rear of her white Ford Escape reached the sidewalk.

"Whoa there!" a man yelled, causing Dee to immediately jam on the brakes. Then she jerked her head to the left, only to see a handsome man about her age, in his late 30s, waving as soon as they made eye contact. He didn't look angry and in fact made a point of approaching the driver's side door to introduce himself: "I'm Samuel Jergen."

"Dee Horst," she told him as she briefly shook hands with him through the vehicle's opened window. "Do you live around here?"

"I . . . live a couple streets over, on Sedona Street, in Desert Highland," Sam replied, looking slightly agitated.

Then he seemed to recover and proceeded to ask Dee, "Where you headed in such a hurry?"

"I'm going to work."

"Are you busy afterward?"

"I don't know," Dee answered. She wasn't sure what else to say because she was so unprepared for the question.

"I'd like to take you out, Dee," Sam told her. "If you're single like me, you want nothing more than a simple dinner date every so often. It's boring sometimes, being alone, even if you like your own company."

"I agree."

"Great! So we can go out tonight, say around seven?"

"I didn't say I . . ."

"Yes you did, Dee," Sam said. "You agreed to go out with me."

Dee was aware she didn't agree to anything, but his pushiness was actually refreshing. She never realized she'd feel this way. She was assuming he was in fact a neighbor, although not one that lived close by. Dee's mother always accused her of being too trusting. Dee simply preferred to "take her chances" on an individual being truthful, rather than immediately raising her hackles. And since her mother, Jolene, had called her on it, Dee was more determined than ever to be trusting.

Sam then said, "I'll be by at seven! You can drive us to the restaurant of your choice and I'll pay. How's that?"

It was impossible for Dee not to nod upon hearing that. She hadn't been on a date in a couple of years. What was so bad about taking a weirdo-neighbor out to dinner, especially since he was paying? Still, why didn't he let Dee pick him up? There was no opportunity for her to ask him that because he seemed to "disappear" just like he'd "appeared." She'd find something to wear for a semi-casual restaurant and await Sam's arrival.

Admittedly Dee was apprehensive about her date because she hadn't gone out with anyone since the end of her five-year engagement, which was a couple years ago. Her ex-fiance had been leading a double life and was eventually given a long prison sentence after pleading guilty to having voluntarily downloaded some illegal material on his personal computer. He had been a co-worker at South-West Web Hosting and had been so easygoing and likable, she'd thought he was marriage material. Obviously she'd been too hopeful about finding someone with whom to share her life (and she didn't want to have to keep paying her mortgage on her own). Dee had purchased her property at a discount as a foreclosure, and it hardly needed any improvements, just some cleaning.

"The date with Sam" was definitely interesting. Sam showed up at seven p.m. on the dot, banging on the front door, ignoring the doorbell. Dee was just putting on her pierced earrings—dangling, sterling silver turquoise—and she gave up finding the hole for the second one because the pounding on the door was so distracting. She ended up removing the one earring, figuring a more simple look was better anyway. Vowing to "keep an open mind" was the only way for Dee to keep from getting irritated. Besides, she was starving and wanted to go out and eat! But she hated dining out alone because it was so awkward.

"I'm coming!" Dee exclaimed when she was in the foyer. She opened the door to see Sam, looking dapper in navy slacks, a tan dress jacket and a multi-colored striped shirt, conservatively unbuttoned at the collar. He was wearing white running shoes, but in his right hand he held a pair of navy loafers that looked expensive.

"Good evening, Dee!" Sam said. "Mind if I change my footwear in your house so I can look slightly more respectable? You look positively stunning, by the way."

"Thank you and come inside," Dee said. She had managed to find "something suitable": a sheer silk, bell-bottomed, lavender jumpsuit with a opened shirt collar and multi-colored buttons. She wore purple sandals with colorful faux jewels, complementing the outfit. She looked good if she did say so, herself.

Sam “got his way” insofar as leaving his running shoes in the foyer, despite the fact Dee figured that was his way of “marking his territory,” so he could spend the night. Also, she’d have to bring him back here, versus taking him home.

Naturally Sam was so phenomenally charming (and he paid for dinner, at “Casa Comida Buena”) Dee wanted him to stay over. But he didn't. She thought she'd made an indication of her approval of him, but he appeared oblivious. Instead he changed back into his running shoes, waved bye and "disappeared" into the night. It was mutually agreed the date was supposed to be platonic, so she had nothing to complain about. Nonetheless, she was frustrated of all things.

Dee took her new stuffed dog into her bedroom and placed it on the left side (when facing it) of the whitewashed, three-drawer dresser. For one reason or another she was seemingly always running late for work and right now needed to get ready. Upon awakening this morning she never could have imagined Sam would show up out of the blue and propose. It was nearly impossible to believe he was here a couple minutes ago, but the proof was the stuffed Cocker Spaniel. She was compelled to pat the dog’s head before going in the bathroom to take a shower. Unnerved by her behavior, it made her wonder if she been alone too long.

As elusive as Sam always was, at least he’d agreed to only be with her and wasn’t interested in dating anyone else. That was very important to Dee. And she took Sam at his word. If he ever said he loved her, she’d know they were on the right track together. She’d been ready to tell him she loved him following their first date, but she was simultaneously wary about telling him that—not because she doubted as much in her heart but because she didn’t want to push him away. It had been very difficult for Dee to remain as aloof as Sam was. Truth be told he'd been like a cat, although not a tom cat, if he'd kept his promise and was monogamous. Sam definitely wanted his own space. Dee identified with as much, which wasn't something she always could have unequivocally stated.

Dee was going to be late if she didn't step on it. So step on it she did, driving to work. At the corner of Invergordon and Casa Blanca she came to a complete stop and took off again, not looking both ways as well as she should have, not unlike the day she was backing out of her driveway and "almost hit" Sam. Not two seconds later, a vehicle hit the left rear of her Escape, surprising the hell out of her.

Once the initial shock subsided, Dee pulled over to the right side of the road, where there was a row of oleander bushes, blocking the view of the upscale property on the other side. That was fine with her; she was embarrassed her vehicle was hit and felt like it was her fault, even if it technically wasn't. However, it may as well have been because the driver of the other vehicle did not pull up behind her and leap out, apologizing profusely. Instead the driver went his or her way and Dee sat there, incredulous. Nonetheless, she recovered quickly because she needed to go to work. Before driving away, she decided to get out and assess the damage.

While Dee was looking at the dent (it wasn't as bad as she'd anticipated), who appeared seemingly out of nowhere but Sam! Dee exclaimed, "Sam! What are you doing here?"

"I left your house and decided to take a long walk," he answered.

"Did you see the guy that hit me?"

"No, I didn't."

"I was hoping I had a witness. He fled the scene."

Eying the damage, Sam remarked, "It looks to me like you got off pretty easy, considering he could have really sideswiped your Escape and hurt you."

"I know it," Dee agreed. "That's why I'm kind of shaken

up. But I'll be all right."

"Where are you headed?"

"To work. Where else this time of the day?"

"It's like déjà vu, Dee," Sam said and laughed. "I love it. The day we'd met you were on your way to work."

Maybe Dee wasn't sufficiently nostalgic because what she took away from the whole scenario was she worked a lot! Meanwhile, Sam was acting strangely, never mind the fact he was pretty far from where he "supposedly" lived. Was he actually just taking a long walk? Did he honestly not have anything better to do? How about getting a job, even if he was wealthy enough not to bother? She already had a pervert for an ex-fiance, so what did she expect, given how trusting she was determined to be?

Dee must have been super-distracted because as she was standing by the left rear of her Escape, Sam walked away and seemed to literally disappear! Not only that she looked at the dent on the vehicle, and it didn't look like more than a tiny scuff mark. In fact, she was pretty sure that mark was there before her Escape was hit.

Not surprisingly Dee couldn't concentrate at work, given how her day had started. Lunchtime couldn't come soon enough, and she took her sack lunch to one of the three metal picnic tables behind the tan concrete block building of South-West Web Hosting. It was in an elevated area that overlooked two-hundred acres of state-owned land. Surrounding the acreage were single-family homes, which meant any wild animals probably lived mostly within the state land. Given how secluded it seemed when Dee was out here alone, she often wondered if a mountain lion or wild boar might decide to join her. The barricade between the patio and the open land consisted of one row of concrete blocks, so there really was no deterrent. On one occasion Dee and her ex-fiance ate lunch out here, and his back was to the acreage. Dee couldn't resist making their lunch more interesting by declaring, "Watch out! Here comes a mountain lion!"

"Shit!" Jerry yelled. Then he leaped up and ran back in the building, blowing right past Dee. So much for him worrying about her welfare, let alone wondering why she too wasn't panicking.

Dee finally couldn't hold in her laughter any longer, and she really let loose. Meanwhile, the back door flew open, and Jerry mocked the sound of Dee's laughter, before closing the door again.

On this particular day, what was to stop Sam from suddenly appearing from somewhere in the desert? Initially that was funny, but the more Dee thought about him, he really was weird, exactly what she thought of him the first time they'd met. If he showed up later with an engagement ring, Dee was going to tell him to keep it, she was happy with the stuffed Cocker Spaniel. And she'd mean it!

Sam didn't "show back up." He was supposed to come back to the house around 6:30, and they were going to spend some private time "reconciling." Afterward they were supposed to go out to dinner. Sam had confessed he hadn't eaten a decent meal since the last time they had gone out together. She found that flattering because it proved (to her) he hadn't been seeing anyone since their amicable breakup. (O.K. She was admittedly weird, too.)

Sam didn't show and didn't show. By nine p.m. Dee was not only starving, she didn't know what the hell to do. He didn't have a cell phone and she was "forbidden" from calling the landline at home, so it was only logical to go where he lived (his mother's house). Since it was late September, it would be dark. It didn't seem like Dee had any choice, and Sam would have to deal with the humiliation he might feel when Dee showed up at his mother's. Dee would explain later, she already knew his living situation before she'd showed up, so he didn't have to feel self-conscious.

The house was beautiful, at least four-thousand square feet, all white stucco, a tall palm tree on either side of it, landscape lighting illuminating the entire property. In front there was a circular driveway, in the middle of which there was a fountain with an angel at the top, a spotlight on it, tipping over a water pail. The garage was perpendicular to Sedona Street, so the entire front of the house was visible, which had floor-to-ceiling windows from the right of the arched front stoop to the end of the house. The white plantation shutters on the windows were closed.

Not to bring up money issues, but obviously Sam really didn't need to work, having a mother who owned a house like this. That said, why did he walk everywhere? Did he have a DUI? Tears were in Dee's eyes when she reached the front doorway. She felt like she "didn't deserve a guy who stood to inherit this place." Admittedly the property wasn't as extravagant as Dee portrayed it, but to actually see where her enigmatic fiancé lived, made the house seem all the more impressive. She was already familiar with the subdivision, so it wasn't like this was a two-block-away culture shock.

Dee wanted nothing more than to use the brass horse head door knocker, but the second she started to do so the door was opened. Before her stood an older woman who looked strikingly similar to Sam. Without bothering to introduce herself, Dee asked her, "Is Sam around?"

The woman (most likely Susan Jergen) looked ready to fall over upon hearing that question. However, she managed to recover and told Dee, "My son's been dead for close to ten years."

It was Dee's turn to fall over and she almost did. Her saving grace was being too shocked to do anything but keep standing there. However, her self-consciousness compelled her to declare, "But Sam proposed to me earlier today!"

Mrs. Jergen shook her head saying, "That's impossible. Samuel killed himself. I had to cut the rope that was around his neck."

"I'm sorry," Dee said. "I didn't come here to upset you. Thank you for your time." Then she turned around and started to leave.

"Wait," Mrs. Jergen said. "Miss . . ."

"Dee Horst," Dee answered, turning back around.

The two women shook hands, which only occurred because Mrs. Jergen stuck out her hand. Dee had so much information to process at the moment, she couldn't think straight.

Mrs. Jergen said, "Dee, come in for a minute. I really should show you something. Please excuse the mess."

Barely had Dee stepped into the black-and-white tiled foyer, and she could see it was lined with every kind of stuffed dog. She felt dizzy and wanted nothing more than to leave again. At the same time she was compelled to stare at all the stuffed dogs.

Meanwhile Mrs. Jergen said, "Samuel keeps coming back. Sometimes he stays for a few days. I leave all the dogs here so he can see them and finally not bring me any more. He knows I'm allergic to dogs and can't have one, so he must think he's doing me a favor, creating a whole collection of stuffed ones. I keep waiting for him to finally rest in peace but it may be a while yet. I hope you have a lot of extra room in your house."

She Stayed for the Dog

Michelle told her husband, Gordon, she needed a minute of his time to talk. They were standing in the kitchen, Gordon having just returned from work. Their dog, Lucifer, a Rottweiler, appeared because it was time for his five p.m. walk. Typically Gordon wore his "work clothes" to walk the dog because he was a personal trainer. Lucifer sure came in handy in that moment. Michelle almost demanded a divorce from her husband of seven years. Although they usually walked Lucifer together, Gordon didn't want to converse while they walked the dog. It took Michelle quite a long time to learn how to shut up because she was naturally pretty talkative, and walking with her dearly beloved compelled her to start yapping. Gordon finally "won" by simply ignoring her when she'd say something or ask him a question. She finally figured out how to keep her mouth shut, by telling herself she was walking with a robot. That sounded ridiculous but it worked!

Grudgingly Gordon stopped long enough to ask Michelle what she needed to talk about before they took Lucifer for a walk, and she told him, "It's nothing, really." Then she felt her face start to burn because he was really looking at her. Did he suspect she was about to tell him she was going to ask for a divorce? Was there a possibility he wanted the same thing? As much as he resembled a human Adonis, there was little else about him to keep her interested. Worse, more and more she had a sneaking suspicion he was cheating on her—and not just occasionally. What was to stop him? He visited his clients' homes in the Phoenix valley, and many of them were females—typically married, no less.

Gordon wasn't too concerned about what Michelle might have wanted to say because he went ahead and put the leash on Lucifer's collar and turned to leave. Finally Michelle couldn't take his robotic attitude anymore and said, "I'm taking a nap," to which Gordon simply nodded and went out the door with Lucifer! Before the dog disappeared from sight, however, he managed to give Michelle "one of those looks." She knew, she knew, she was giving the dog too much credit, but she still believed the dog was trying to tell her something.

Ascending the staircase to the master bedroom, Michelle was suddenly so exhausted she could hardly move her legs. What was going on? She wasn't the health nut Gordon was, but she took excellent care of herself and usually felt energetic. She looked forward to walking Lucifer with her husband, even if he made a point of ignoring her the entire duration.

When Michelle laid down, she fell asleep right away. Although she awoke at some point and wanted to get up and make dinner, she went right back to sleep! It wasn't like Gordon was difficult to cook for; he liked raw vegetables with dressing dip as an appetizer. The main course could never be anything fried, and he didn't like sauce "covering up the real taste of something." Michelle often considered the possibility perhaps Gordon was afraid to eat something tasty, or he'd be unable to control himself and in turn over-indulge. A few dozen times of "pigging out," and his six-pack abs might have a sheen of fat over them. Michelle wasn't about to deride her husband for wanting a perfect body; he'd said it himself more than once, his body was his best advertisement for the business he ran with his partner, Jesse Matthews. He was "the guy behind the scenes" and was too busy doing all the bookwork to stay in shape. His paunch was hidden behind the desk he sat at for most of his work day.

Maybe it was "the seven-year itch" of her marriage, but

lately Michelle felt as if Gordon's and her relationship had really stagnated. Why else would she have been compelled to tell him she wanted a divorce? The suspicion he repeatedly cheated on her didn't bother her as much as the fact she felt entirely "blah" about him.

Michelle not only fell back to sleep, she slept until the next morning—and it was already daylight! Having awoken with a start, she immediately looked over at where Gordon slept. He was already up, and his two pillows were scrunched, so he must have spent the night next to her. How understanding of him, to let her get the extra rest she'd obviously needed.

Then Michelle heard the shower water running. Gordon must not have gotten up too much earlier, so she took advantage of that and got up to make him breakfast. Since she failed to make him dinner last evening, she had to do something to redeem herself. She'd fallen asleep in her clothes from the day before, so she would change from her shirt and jeans to another pair of jeans and a shirt.

Breakfast was one meal Gordon did indulge in (sort of). Pancakes smothered with blueberry jam was his favorite. He didn't mind if Michelle used pancake mix versus making the pancakes "from scratch," so she went ahead and started making breakfast. Feeling like someone was watching her, she turned around to see Lucifer, looking in the French door. Gordon had let him out after feeding him breakfast. The whole backyard was fenced with wrought iron, but Michelle still worried a coyote could get in. Gordon would tell her it was impossible a coyote could take out a Rottweiler. She never got past the notion her husband had already accepted the fact the two animals would be in a fight, and there would probably be a lot of blood. She would have said Gordon was just being funny, but he had practically no sense of humor. Again, she went back to her desire to ask him for a divorce. It was only logical to feel frustrated enough to do so!

Michelle let Lucifer in so he could sit at her feet while she continued making breakfast. Meanwhile, she got to thinking about the early going of her marriage, and Gordon was always into her. She hadn't expected that intensity of emotion to last "forever," and it didn't. In the past six months Gordon's affection had disappeared altogether. It was bad enough Michelle was given the silent treatment whenever they walked Lucifer, but Gordon had stopped kissing her good-bye before leaving for work at "Body Perfect," a health and fitness establishment. Gordon also made "house calls," so that was how the issue about him having affairs, came in. It was pure speculation on her part, but he seemed bored out of his mind with her. She couldn't say she blamed him. She bored herself, sometimes.

As far as a kiss from Gordon when he returned from work? He had never given her one, the entire seven years of their marriage. Michelle had plenty of time to think about Gordon's side of the situation, and she decided it was all part of a well-thought out plan of his. In other words he knew she'd smell or notice something if she got too close to him after he'd been working so hard all day. What a joke. It was said if you loved what you did you never worked a day in your life, and that fit Gordon's livelihood to a T. He was obsessed with fitness and enjoyed preaching the benefits of exercise and healthy eating. His physical attractiveness helped make him a walking advertisement for his and his partner's business. Michelle used to get irritated by her husband's single-mindedness—until he started bringing home so much money she quit her job. She was a receptionist at a very busy real estate company, and she'd been ready to quit for some time, having long ago realized she was underpaid for how much work she did. Fortunately she didn't sit around at home and become lazy and fat. Otherwise Gordon probably would have left her. Admittedly Michelle was petrified of living alone—not in the physical sense per se but definitely in the emotional sense. Did that even make any sense?

Gordon appeared, dressed for work in his navy sweatpants, a white polo shirt and a brand-new pair of white athletic shoes. He looked so good this morning Michelle couldn't believe he was real. Ridiculous of course. She needed to appreciate the fact she was still attracted to him even if there was nothing else to be said in his favor!

"How are you feeling, darling?" Gordon asked as he sat down.

Michelle replied, "I'm better than I was last night. I'd never been so exhausted." Meanwhile she poured him a cup of coffee. It was a strong brew, and he drank it black. "Thanks for letting me sleep, although I wanted to get up and make dinner. I'm sorry. I don't know what happened."

"You looked so peaceful, I couldn't wake you, anyway."

"What did you do about dinner?" she couldn't help asking. He didn't cook, period.

"I . . . went to 'Ciao's' and picked up a pasta salad."

"Did you bring it home to eat it?"

"I ate in my car, just outside the carry-out place, if you really need to know," Gordon replied, sounding quite irritated. His expression, however, was blank of all things. Maybe he was so mad he had no expression at all.

Gordon's coffee was served to him, and he looked like he needed the coffee just to continue functioning! The joking about him being a robot aside, he looked exactly like one.

Michelle waited a few seconds to see if Gordon would even notice the steaming hot cup of coffee in front of him before finally saying, "Here's your coffee, honey."

"Oh," Gordon said, appearing to "snap out of it."

Perhaps the long hours Gordon worked, were taking a toll on him. Nonetheless, he would never slow down. He'd have to break down, first, really break – like a robot. She kept going back to that, which was really funny!

Gordon drank his coffee, as in the whole cup and it was scalding hot. He liked it that way but usually only sipped it.

Michelle said, "I'll get you another cup of coffee after I flip the pancakes." Then she hurried over to the stove. Gordon didn't like pancakes that were too dark, even on one side. He'd refuse to eat them, which would really tick her off. That wasn't important, save for the fact she was already mad at him. It was one of those situations in which he was the one who was (probably) cheating on her, hence instigating the conflict. However, she was the one who would end up getting in trouble.

After flipping the pancakes, Michelle went to retrieve Gordon's empty coffee cup and stopped in horror: he looked like he was paralyzed. Did he have a seizure? He'd never had any health problems she was aware of. She kept looking at him, unsure what to do. He had to still be breathing, or he'd slide off the chair, wouldn't he? So he was probably in some sort of trance. He put in too many hours for work, but Michelle's sympathy was limited, given his possible extracurricular activities.

Maybe it was due to shock, but Michelle felt calm when she went ahead and refilled Gordon's coffee cup and placed it before him. Then she stood there again, staring at him. His eyes were open, but it didn't appear he could see anything. She couldn't decide if that was reassuring or she needed to panic.

"Gordon, are you all right?" Michelle asked, her voice quivering. "Gordon honey, can you hear me?" Then she said his name several more times, sounding more and more plaintive with each utterance.

Just as Michelle was about to collapse in tears, Gordon abruptly sat up ramrod straight and looked around like he'd been unconscious or asleep. Afterward he zeroed in on Michelle and appeared to need a couple seconds to recognize her. Again, she couldn't figure out if she should be relieved or more freaked out. Then he said, "Thanks for the refill. I'm starving. Is breakfast about ready?"

Gordon wasn't much for words, if the fact he didn't want to talk while they walked Lucifer, wasn't enough proof. Therefore, if he was waiting for breakfast, he'd just sit there.

Not to bring up the robot allusion yet again, but he sounded exactly like one when he'd said that!

"It should be ready right now," Michelle replied, glad to have something to do for a minute: serve her robot breakfast! Inwardly she laughed at her joke, but there was nothing laughable going on, after all. The ultimate proof? Lucifer had been sitting right in the middle of the kitchen as she'd been getting things ready, even sitting at her feet at times, yet he was nowhere to be seen – for some time already. Michelle admittedly lost track of his whereabouts ever since all this weirdness with Gordon, began. Had it been going on longer than she thought? Was that why Lucifer had been giving her "one of those looks"? Had he been doing so for longer than she was aware? That was certainly possible. Suddenly it didn't seem strange at all, Lucifer might "know something." That was a lot more reasonable than the contention Gordon might be a robot.

After scarfing down the pancake breakfast, Gordon leaped up and left for work. Just like that. Usually he brushed his teeth first. Initially she thought he'd jogged to Body Perfect, but he at least still had enough sense to drive there in his white Chevy Tahoe. (It was about a half-marathon's length away.) Even though Gordon was fit enough to jog there, he'd have nothing left to get through his day, especially if he had to make a couple house calls. Those alone would deplete him, and he wouldn't have enough energy to jog back home at the end of the day. As it was, he appeared to be "running on empty."

Gordon's departure compelled Lucifer to emerge from the utility room. He only hid there during a severe thunderstorm, a rarity here in Arizona. Michelle was so unnerved by all these strange happenings involving Gordon, she gave Lucifer a hug. She had to hug a dog to feel "normalcy"? Yes. And now that she was doing so much wondering, she'd have to do some investigating. She thought she'd have to spy on her husband to catch him cheating, but it was going to be a more "involved" investigation than that: to conclude if her husband was real! That sounded so absurd, but it proved life really was stranger than fiction.

Typically Gordon went to Body Perfect early enough in the morning to have time to meet with his partner, Jesse, and do some brainstorming. Even though the latter ran the company, Gordon was the one who offered the most input regarding day-to-day operations. Between the two of them they ran a money-making venture, which never ceased to amaze Michelle. She was glad she didn't have to work ever again.

Like many other fitness establishments, Body Perfect was housed in a building whose entire front was floor to ceiling windows. Inside there were stationary bicycles, some treadmills and a few weight machines. It sounded like the "perfect" place to spy on someone, but Michelle would have to be discreet about it. Wearing a disguise would help, too. However, rather than rush over there, she needed a plan.

Then again, why didn't she leave well enough alone? Michelle asked herself as much while again considering how well Gordon provided for her (and Lucifer), having also just mentioned how she no longer had to bother working. So what if he did cheat on her and was a robot, to boot? That wasn't a joke, which was good because it wasn't funny, despite her earlier claim.

What Michelle and Lucifer needed right now was to unwind. That meant a walk was in order. He appeared to enjoy walks as much as she did, and they were soon out the door.

Passing the well-kept yards in the neighborhood, Lucifer couldn't get enough of sniffing and looking around, and Michelle was less stressed, simply by seeing her dog enjoy himself. Nonetheless she couldn't help thinking about Gordon. Exactly what was going on with him?

After Michelle and Lucifer went around one block, she decided they needed a longer walk and they went around another block before heading home.

"You should have alerted me sooner you were having problems," Jesse admonished Gordon, upon the latter's appearance in his office at Body Perfect. It was only 8:30 a.m. but the place was busy with customers working out. "Lock the door and have a seat. We need to take care of you."

What a mess this whole thing could be if Jesse wasn't careful. It had started out as a "brilliant experiment," borne of the fact his brother, Leon, worked for the Pentagon. Jesse wasn't bragging, merely proving the feasibility of the following: Gordon Turner was an extremely life-like robot! There weren't more than two dozen of these "people" running around in the world, and Jesse had one of them to help run his fitness business. Gordon was so "real" Jesse referred to him as his partner.

The biggest problem was the fact Gordon was married. Jesse had him until 2030 "if everything worked out." After that, who knew? Gordon's brother was never clear about what happened after that. If nothing else Jesse would sell the business and retire. He'd be pretty well-set financially in another few years. As for Michelle, Gordon's wife, she would eventually be forced to face the fact she wasn't married to an actual person. It was possible she wouldn't be able to cope with that realization, but there was no reason to worry about as much for the time being. At least, that was how it appeared, since everything had been going along so well.

Gordon (and Jesse) was lucky Michelle didn't want kids and was content to take care of a dog. Jesse sometimes wished he'd married a gal like her versus his wife, Suzanne, with whom he had two rug rats. They were one year apart, both in their early teens . . . If he could do it over again . . .

"At least you're in here now," Jesse told a comatose-looking Gordon. "Given what you told me about possibly 'temporarily losing your connection,' that would be like a person losing consciousness, although you claim you didn't. What did you say you ate for breakfast? You mumbled it the first time."

"Pancakes with blueberry jam!" Gordon exclaimed.

"We already agreed you weren't going to eat that ever again! You're going to need a clean-out."

"I passed on Michelle's pancakes at least once because she got them too dark on one side. That's my excuse for not eating them. She got them right this morning. What was I supposed to do?"

Jesse didn't say anything and instead grabbed the metal wastepaper basket in the corner and kneeled before Gordon, who'd turned his chair around. Difficult though it was, Jesse needed to find the elusive spot of "the stomach latch." The cost of a service call made it "worth it" to look for the damned thing. Airfare alone for the technician was a significant expense, as he flew in from Washington, D.C., first class, "for security reasons."

There was a knock on the (locked) door. Never in all the years this place had been open, had a customer knocked on the office door, locked or unlocked (typically the latter). The point was, why today of all days? Jesse couldn't ignore the person knocking. Since he had yet to find the latch, it was better to crack open the door and deal with whoever was there.

If Michelle had a tail it would have been between her legs as she exited Body Perfect, given what she'd just witnessed. Although she caught no more than a glimpse of what was going on inside Jesse Matthews' office, she could draw her own conclusion and be right. She always thought she was good at assuming and "being right" while doing so. This was what she deserved for just walking in the place, thinking she was going to confront Gordon. Doing so was the opposite of her earlier resolution to have a plan/leave well enough alone.

Jesse and Gordon were lovers, so what, after all? Michelle had already made it clear, she wasn't going anywhere, at least as long as Lucifer was alive. Maybe she was too lazy to look for an apartment that allowed dogs.

Outsiders

The year was 2320. You only lived on "The Outside" of any city if you wanted to live like people used to. Otherwise you lived in one of a couple dozen "major cities" in the United States, and there was a twenty-foot high concrete wall surrounding each one's downtown. Urban sprawl no longer existed. Over half the country's population was wiped out by a deadly flu virus, and "the family dog" was the only carrier. "The blame" on the epidemic wasn't placed on dogs at the onset, yet almost every citizen in the country happened to own at least one dog.

Once a vaccine was finally available to stop the flu epidemic, most of the remaining population was so shell shocked by the fact "dogs" caused the disaster, they were permanently banned as pets within the walled cities. It made no difference an effective vaccine stopped the epidemic, and there was absolutely no chance a dog could infect another person EVER AGAIN. Anyone who lived in the walled cities didn't believe this, but the "Outsiders" knew otherwise and/or were willing to take their chances.

Tara Millsten was one of the "Outsiders" and proud of it. Not only that, she and her husband, Daryl, thrived on the open spaces available ever since the population had abruptly shrunk. Tara dared to call the city dwellers "scaredy-cats" because they not only were scared to own a dog (nor allowed to) but could not take in any of the feral cats running around the cities. Of course people did anyway, but if you were caught . . . you'd never be seen again. That was how high paranoia ran in the cities, that cats were potentially the next carriers of a deadly flu epidemic. Logically you would wonder why the government didn't just wipe out the cat population as a "preventative measure," but that would have caused massive riots. Instead, it appeared to be easier to let the cats roam around the walled cities, although their numbers didn't increase too dramatically because they were trapped, "fixed," and released again.

The effort the government went to, to keep everyone "happy" within the country's walled cities, was something Tara found very amusing. Her sister, Tamara Christopher, happened to live in a walled Chicago, Illinois. The majestic skyscraper in which she resided with her husband and two children was home to other "successful people," and Tamara's family lived on the 90th story, in a penthouse formerly reserved just for them. However, they had to turn over the separate apartments for their maid and nanny, who had lived on the 89th floor, so other residents could move in. Fortunately Tamara's husband, Craig, made a very good living, or simply handing over two one-bedroom apartments to the powers that be would have been a huge financial strain.

What Tara would have given to be even slightly like Tamara, but they were practically polar opposites. The "biggest similarity" was the fact they were identical twins. For all Tara knew, Tamara wished she were more like her sister, but she'd never let on about it. You'd think after everything that had taken place, Tamara would have been at least slightly more personable. She was the one with two kids, teens at this point, but still. And they definitely had it made; the school they attended was in the basement of the building they lived in!

Tamara never appeared to tire of telling Tara how well her husband (Tamara's) was doing financially. Having money was always extremely important to her, and it probably had to do with the fact their parents, Anita and Dwight, gave their daughters a very comfortable upbringing.

As for the elder Snells, both had succumbed to the dog flu, having caught it from their German shepherd, Astro. Also, Anita Snell's mother, Rhonda, passed away from it, thanks to Ralph, her Jack Russell terrier.

Sometimes it was infuriating how insulated Tamara pretended to be. Maybe Tara was such an "Outsider" by this point in time, she simply couldn't relate to someone who lived in a walled city, not even her identical sister. Tara's issue was she could really use a friend, and her sister should have been the logical choice. This wasn't to say she didn't consider her husband, Daryl, a friend. Maybe he was a lover first and not much else. Maybe she was bored (but she'd never cheat on him, she loved him too much). And he was so honest it was impossible he'd ever stray. Tara was lucky to have married such a great man. If he had a fault it was his tendency to work too much and refuse to relax. It was probably a coping mechanism, given how much everyone's lives had changed since the dog flu decimated the country.

Coincidentally Tamara called Tara's mobile phone just after the latter had filled the water buckets for six horses (used mostly for herding Daryl's 500 beef cattle). He was nowhere to be seen, as he was on Sugar, an old gray Quarter horse mare, checking the fences. Tara and he had a thousand acres in western Iowa.

Tamara never was much for introductions, and this morning was no different. Then she blew Tara's mind, asking, "Could you come here? I need to talk to you about something . . . I know it's almost a day's drive, but if you leave right now you'll get here before they lock the city up for the night."

Immediately Tara's heart went out to her sister, but it wasn't long before her defenses went back up. She told Tamara, "I hate to just take off. Daryl is out checking fences, and he didn't take his phone. He never does because he can't get a signal."

"Call him when you get here," Tamara told Tara, sounding way too eager and helpful. Something was wrong, for sure.

"I'd like to bring Mouse, but I'll never get in," Tara said, referring to her black Labrador retriever. "I guess I could park outside and start home again after we talk."

"You won't want to leave him in your truck all night."

"Tamara, I just told you I won't be able to stay."

"Fine! Just come here now and leave the damned dog at home! They're the ones who caused all this anyway," Tamara said and started crying.

"As soon as I finish my chores I'll be on my way," Tara declared, although she didn't "feel convinced" about what she was about to do.

"You did a good job, Tam," Craig told his wife while holding a .38 to her head. "You sounded convincing and now your @ % # & sister is coming here. I'd warned you I'd go stir crazy if I couldn't leave this place. It's all your fault so you get to pay." Then he shot her. Not a sound was heard, thanks to an (illegal) silencer. What the flip wasn't illegal anymore, especially in this once-wonderful city? Craig's life had been turned upside-down by the dog flu, and his family was one of the few in the country who didn't even own one! He lost his in-laws to it, his parents, two sisters . . . He couldn't even list everyone who no longer was or he'd start crying. That was the last thing he wanted to do because he had to stay strong for his kids, although at ages fourteen and fifteen, they should have been about ready to live on their own. Nonetheless, Tamara would go to the basement of their apartment building and wait for them at the end of the school day. (The classrooms were in the apartment building itself.) Then she'd ride the elevator with them back up to their penthouse apartment. Most days that was the only time she left. Even though there was a supermarket right in the building as well, she had their maid do the grocery shopping. It was amazing what the dog flu had done to the mindset of the population.

What Craig just did to his wife was 100% premeditated, but he had absolutely no fear of getting caught and in turn tried and found guilty. This country had enough to do, just trying to help keep everyone sane. Meanwhile Craig was going to seduce his sister-in-law because she had way more spunk than his wife—even when Tamara was alive! It gave him something to do, and maybe he too had gone insane. And Tara, his sister-in-law, was an identical twin, so this could not only give him something to do but he could have some fun, watching everyone fall for his ruse.

Tara made good time driving to Chicago and she was proud of herself. At the last second she almost brought Mouse, despite the irrationality of doing so. She'd have to park on the outside of the city wall because of him, and it was possible someone would steal him. In turn he would be smuggled into the city. The irony was confounding.

Mouse meant too much to Tara to hope he was safe in her truck for even an hour or two. She'd found his pregnant mother, abandoned by the side of a rural road near home. It was long after the worst of the dog flu epidemic had subsided, yet dogs were still unpopular even with "Outsiders." Once "Missy" had her puppies, however, there was a demand for them. Tara sold Mouse's four siblings for as much as five grand apiece. Even taking inflation into account, that was quite a steep price. The buyers were in fact insistent Tara take the money because there were so few purebred dogs available.

Just as Tara parked her truck in a large, paved parking lot on the west side of Chicago, a couple hundred yards from a gated, walk-through entrance, her cell phone rang. She preferred taking the call in the relative safety of her vehicle. Anymore, petty crime was rampant just outside the walls of all the cities in the United States, particularly just outside any walk-through entrances. There were four of those, yet only one entrance for vehicles. That was about a thousand yards from where she was parked. The last thing she wanted to do was be distracted while she was walking, simultaneously talking on her phone.

The caller was Daryl, who skipped any sort of greeting and screamed, "I just read your note and Mouse is sitting here whining. How could your selfish sister need you more than we do?"

Tara felt so ashamed! She really hadn't thought all this through well enough. Daryl had a right to be upset, and he never was unless he had a good reason. She told him, "She probably doesn't. I'm sorry I just took off like I did. She sounded so desperate, I jumped at her bidding."

"Come home now, please?" Daryl pleaded.

"Tamara had told me she had something to tell me and she could only do so in person," Tara said, recalling aloud how all this started.

"Too bad!" Daryl cried. "If you haven't gone in the city yet, which I'm assuming you haven't, just stay out of the place. Too many 'Outsiders' are going in and not ever coming back out. Delivery people are about the only ones who are relatively safe, and they're forced to wear Hazmat suits, just to keep the peace."

Looking around the parking lot, which had at least five hundred spaces, there weren't more than two dozen vehicles in it. At least six of them were gritty-looking, as if they'd been parked there for a few months. Granted, there were four or five of these parking areas on the outside of the city, but if it was really such a great place to visit, wouldn't every parking lot be relatively full?

Tara hated to admit she was afraid – for her sister and herself. She told her husband, "I feel like I can't just leave again, now that I drove all this way."

"Call her and make her come outside to see you."

"There isn't much time before the gates are locked for the night, but that's a really good idea. Then she can pay for the cab ride."

"Do that and call me back, would you?"

"Yes, I will," Tara replied. "I love you."

Tara was sure Daryl said he loved her too, but the connection had broken up.

Immediately Tara called Tamara's cell phone, as she answered that instead of the land line. This time around, however, it rang and rang, to the point Tara was about to end the call when Tamara's husband, Craig, answered, saying, "Tara? It's Craig. Are you outside the building?"

Rather than directly answer her brother-in-law (who was very arrogant, just like his wife), Tara asked him, "Could I please talk to Tamara?"

"She's taking a nap."

"Could you put Chris or Gail on?" Tara asked, suspicious something was terribly wrong. At the very least Tamara's two kids ought to have been around, if everything was "O.K."

"They're with a neighbor-friend for dinner tonight," Craig answered. "Tamara and I have been enjoying some 'alone-time,' if you know what I mean. Again, I ask, are you outside the building? Security can buzz you in because I already cleared you."

Tara didn't like the sound of that at all. The last thing she intended to do was reveal she was sitting in her truck, parked in a huge paved lot on the west exterior side of the city, the closest one to the only vehicle entrance. Craig would sick a couple of his goon-friends on her, following her in her truck and running her down. Whatever happened to her sister, Tara would never know because she was officially an "Outsider."

Money for Nothing

Two thousand grand, cash, a week for twelve weeks, amounted to twenty-four thousand dollars! Allison Burr never was good in math (or any other subject in school), but she was when it involved something worthwhile. In this case it did, but she'd have to work for the money. Or to put it another way: she'd have to be a nanny for another twelve weeks, and it was a profession she'd been trying to get away from. She'd lasted being one for close to ten years, so it couldn't have been too unbearable. What helped in that regard was she happened to work for people who had a lot of money. That didn't mean they all paid well, however. Some who appeared to be the most well-off, paid the worst. Nonetheless, Allison's living arrangements never failed to be above average. Sometimes she actually cried when a family no longer needed her because she liked their house (or guest house) so much.

This job was a last-minute kind of thing, and if it wasn't for the excellent pay, Allison would have passed it up. She had been recommended by her best friend, Sheila Cross, who was taking a leave of absence to care for her mother, who was recuperating from a serious car accident injury. At one point Sheila wasn't even on speaking terms with her mother, but they must have patched up their differences. If Allison hadn't agreed to fill in for her friend, she would have been sitting around her parents' house in Evansville, Indiana, trying to decide what to do with herself next. It wasn't usual for her to be "home," so she long ago gave up renting an apartment. Her parents, Joe and Cindy, didn't mind their only child crashing at their house between jobs, as they rarely saw her, not even for Christmas.

What Allison needed most right now was to replace her maroon Nissan Sentra with something that had newer tires and less miles on the odometer. Therefore, the first thing some of the money from this "last nanny gig" would go to was a decent used car. Next, some of it would go toward getting an education for a new job skill. As much as she liked feeling as if she was living the high life, residing in rich people's houses (or the guest house behind the main house) didn't delude her. She needed to build a life for herself, not keep going home to her parents' between jobs.

One reason Allison wanted to leave her career as a nanny was she endured a huge come-on from a former employer. At the same time she was afraid to reject his advances, in case he in turn fired her. He didn't but she was nonetheless angry. It felt like she'd been taken advantage of, in a certain regard. It was tempting to tell the guy's wife about her husband's lack of class, but she was probably already aware of as much, having been married to him for a dozen years.

Allison had relative youth on her side at twenty-nine, but she was not a supermodel in the looks department. Since she already interviewed for this latest job, she met "the wife," and she was very attractive. Sheila claimed the woman's husband was rarely around, as he lived and worked in Manhattan. This twelve week "assignment" would be on a farm in Lexington, Kentucky. Husband would possibly visit, but if nothing else he'd "show up at the end to pay her" (meaning Allison). In the meantime she'd be given cash for "necessities." Allison was welcome to eat meals with "the family," which included the Coaten's daughter, Stella. Allison could eat alone or with a family of twelve, and she liked to think she was naturally very adaptive.

In the morning Allison would be leaving her parents' place and driving to her new job, about three hours away.

Her mother would make sure Allison had breakfast first, knowing her daughter didn't like to bother cooking for herself. It wasn't in any contract Allison had to cook for a family, but she usually ended up doing so – not every meal but sometimes it seemed like it. The parents would be off somewhere, if there was a cook he or she was gone for the day, and the kids would look up at her like she was supposed to snap her fingers and make dinner appear.

The lady Allison would be working for, Sarah, supposedly liked to cook and had taken a cooking class to make sure she was halfway decent. However, her admitted weakness was an obsession with horses. She supposedly competed them in something or the other, but she was recovering from an injury following a bad fall and was only able to "flat them," whatever that meant. Sarah wanted her daughter in the barn as much as possible once she turned four, but fortunately the girl was only three. Allison would be long gone before that would be a concern, at least she hoped. She was afraid of horses and preferred to stay as far away from them as possible, even if they were locked up in a stall.

Allison's aged car made the trip a second time, on this occasion "for real," and it actually "died" when it was about ten feet from where she'd intended to park it, on the right side of the beautiful house's wraparound porch. Sarah had told her the house was 6,000 square feet when Allison first met her. Allison really only saw the kitchen, where the two had sat in the spacious "breakfast nook" for Allison's interview. From what little Allison had seen of the house, what wasn't spacious?

As Allison was about to get out of her "broken" car, what appeared but a big, black wooly dog! Allison hadn't seen that thing the last time she was here. The proof? She never would have agreed to take this job, no matter how much money she was supposed to be paid. She never saw enough of the house to spy the thing's water bowl. Nor had Sheila mentioned a word about the dog. Come to think of it she was vague about a lot of things, purposefully or not. Maybe Allison didn't really know her very well, despite assuming she did.

Rather than get out of the car, Allison called Sarah's cell phone, and of course she didn't answer. Just as Allison was ready to leave again (but realized her car was kaput), Sarah appeared. Meanwhile, the stupid dog kept circling her car. What Allison would have given to have backed up and run the dog over.

Grabbing the dog's collar, Sarah said, "Don't be afraid of Bear, Allison. I had him at the groomer's getting a bath when you were here last time. He lives in the barn, so he won't be any concern of yours."

"I'm afraid of dogs," Allison couldn't help saying, despite the fact it was unnecessary.

Bear was dragged all the way to the barn while he kept looking at Allison's car (or Allison?) and was reluctant to depart. She didn't like that sight at all, nor was she reassured by Sarah having told her the dog lived in the barn. Obviously he was free to roam around the property. Allison had no intention of hiding in the house for twelve weeks, but maybe that wasn't such a bad idea. She'd have more money to take with her at the end, since she wouldn't even have to go out shopping for personal items. That sounded ridiculous, but Allison absolutely did not want to have to face that dog. Having it repeatedly circle her car had renewed a deep fear of dogs. Not only that, it was safe to say that one already had her figured out.

Finally Allison got out and unloaded the trunk of her car. She managed to carry everything to the front entryway in one trip, although she'd brought quite a few bags.

Allison had never met her "charge," three-year-old Stella, as she had been taking a nap when Allison was interviewed. Anyway, none other than Stella was on the other side of the storm door, appearing to be waiting for her new nanny.

Since Stella made no motion to open the storm door, Allison greeted her from the exterior of it and asked, "May I come in, Stella?"

"How do you know my name?" Stella wanted to know. "What's yours?"

"I'm Allison. Your mother and I talked and she's letting me work here for a little bit."

Sarah then called from the barn, "Go ahead in the house, Allison, I'll be there in a minute and show you your suite."

Allison liked how her living quarters were described. This job could end up feeling like a vacation. Already she wasn't concerned about her broken down car or the dog—for the time being, at least.

The second floor suite did not disappoint. The private bath had a whirlpool tub with a window overlooking the east side of the Coaten's farm and the hilly countryside beyond. The queen-sized bed had a colorfully-patterned quilt, which matched the throw rug at the foot of the bed. There was a wood floor, but the bathroom had white tile. The suite was "country chic," as Allison would have described it. She positively loved it and didn't mind the fact there didn't appear to be a TV anywhere. However, it turned out it was in a green-colored, wooden entertainment console that resembled a small armoire, facing the sitting area to the right of the bed. So she could sit in a comfortable chair or lay in bed to watch television. Did Sheila have any idea what she was missing? She never mentioned if she'd worked for the Coatens long enough to make this southerly trek.

Usually Allison was pretty reserved in regard to exhibiting enthusiasm, but on this occasion she couldn't hide how much she liked her new digs and told Sarah as much.

"Glad to hear it," Sarah said.

"Did you do the decorating?" Allison asked.

"Yes, I did."

Then Stella appeared, just as Allison was about to tell her new boss she ought to consider a career in decorating. That cute little girl came in handy. Otherwise Allison would have had to put her foot in her mouth, as there was no need to tell her new boss what to do with her life. It was anyone's guess if Allison would be welcome to stay long enough to start her new job, had she offered her unsolicited opinion.

"What is it, honey?" Sarah asked her daughter.

"I'm hungry," Stella replied. "Are you making something for lunch?"

"I'll make sandwiches for the three of us. How's that?"

"O.K."

"'O.K.' That's it?" Sarah said and laughed. "I'll get lunch ready while Allison puts her things away. Come and help me, kiddo."

Sarah and Stella departed, and Allison was never so relieved to have a few minutes to herself, to unpack and think. As nice as Sarah Coaten seemed to be (as well as her daughter, Stella) SOMETHING WASN'T RIGHT. Maybe it had to do with the big, wooly dog named Bear. Allison wasn't sure if she should be "relieved" the dog was potentially the issue.

The remainder of the day was uneventful. Never was Allison one to appreciate as much, but she did on this occasion. In the meantime she felt like she'd aged thirty years, she was so anxious.

Sarah had to run into town (Georgetown in this case) and pick up a few things. This meant Allison had her first official "time alone with Stella." Barely had "Mom" exited the farm in her white Range Rover when Stella asked, "Can I please go to the barn?"

"No," Allison stated.

"I'm bored."

All Allison could think was, Stella Coaten was way too young to say something like that. She had to be parroting her mother. Rather than accuse Stella of as much, Allison said, "I hate the word 'bored,' to be honest."

"Can I go to the barn, please?" Stella asked again, as if she never heard Allison's "No."

Allison felt a cold sweat breaking out under her arms. That only happened when she was super-stressed. This kid was more than a handful; she was a total head game and was winning already. However, Allison attempted to remain calm and told Stella, "Your mother doesn't want you to go there yet. I'm sure she has plenty of valid reasons." She almost gave away the "fourth birthday rule" but feared Stella would claim TODAY was her b-day. Stella was obviously old enough (even if she wasn't yet four) to be aware it was necessary to go to the barn if she wanted any time with her mother.

Allison's cell phone rang, which provided a great distraction, so she didn't have to be coerced by a precocious three-year-old, staring, arms folded, appearing ready to throw a tantrum. Allison had dealt with plenty of temper tantrums in the span of her career.

The caller was Sarah, who didn't even say "hi" and launched right into telling Allison, "Do not take Stella to the barn, no matter how much she howls!"

Joking aside, it was plain Sarah was entirely serious, and Allison assured her she wouldn't cave to Stella's desires. In the meantime Allison happened to look away from where Stella was standing. Not more than a few seconds later Allison looked back at Stella, and she was no longer there! Allison practically hung up on her new boss, saying, "I have to go now. Stella just got out of my line of sight."

It felt like Allison's heart was going to beat right out of her chest, as she looked around the first floor of the house, expecting to see Stella—but not seeing her. It was impossible she flew out the door. There would have been a noise of some sort.

Allison honestly had no idea where to go next. Upstairs? Was it possible Stella would hide under Allison's bed? Or maybe Stella would hide under her own bed. Rather than entertain either possibility Allison determined the best place to start looking for Stella was in the barn.

The second Allison was standing on the porch, she wanted to go back inside, realizing she might be noticed by the dog. She forced herself to focus on her responsibility of keeping an eye on Stella at all times and "at any cost."

After making sure the main door didn't automatically lock once it was closed, she shut it, as well as the storm door, and slowly walked in the direction of the barn. It happened to look further away than - before. Before what? Before she knew there was a dog that claimed the whole farm as its "territory." Never mind Sarah telling her the thing lived in the barn.

Allison's legs were shaking by the time she found herself standing in the half-opened doorway of the brown steel barn. It looked completely dark inside, even though it was the middle of the day and the late spring sun was warm and bright. Allison shivered.

There was a rustling somewhere down the concrete aisle, but it was probably one of the horses in its stall. Sarah said she had four horses "right now" but the barn had eight stalls. Rather than waltz down the aisle, Allison said, "Stella? It's me, Allison. Are you in here? If you are, could you do me a huge favor and come out from wherever you're hiding? Your mom is going to be home again soon, and the last thing I'm sure she wants to find out, is you decided to sneak out here without permission and then hide."

Once Allison realized she was nervously blathering, she stopped herself—and wanted to run back to the house. However, she had a feeling Stella was indeed hiding in the barn, thinking it was "funny" to do so.

Michael Coaten had a surprise for his wife, Sarah: he was going to pay an overnight visit to their Lexington farm. A friend of his was giving him a free ride on his chartered jet. It was only one-way, however. Michael would have to foot the bill for his return trip to New York. The occasion for his friend's generosity? Michael's 50th birthday. And his daughter Stella's fourth birthday was in a couple days, so they could both celebrate. The surprise was for Sarah first and foremost because she was always lonely and "stuck in

Kentucky" as she described her situation, yet she was aware Michael's job in New York was what paid for their comfortable lifestyle. (She would argue she had money before meeting him. True. But they had lots more now.) And she was the one who'd inherited the Kentucky farm and refused to sell it. So she had her horses shipped here from Weston, Connecticut, where Michael and she had a lovely house. There she boarded her horses at a hundred-stall stable a couple miles down the road. The place always made room for her, as she sometimes had as many as six horses. Right now she only had four, he was pretty sure. There was no disputing it, Sarah was obsessed with horses. The extent of Michael's interest in them was knowing she was too busy with them to have any time for an extramarital affair. Michael had long ago finished "sleeping around" by the time he first laid eyes on his future wife. Forty-four at the time, he had been forced to believe in love at first sight, skeptic though he was until then.

Once Michael was close to the farm, he figured he'd call Sarah and let her know he was "almost there." She'd laugh and never believe he was close by. Honestly he couldn't wait to see her; she'd driven down to Lexington close to three weeks ago, meeting the horse van driver in front of the barn. The guy had arrived before her because she had been delayed, thanks to prolonging her good-bye. Meanwhile Michael had made record time commuting to New York City, feeling stupendous, despite the fact he might not see his wife for as long as twelve weeks—unless he managed to tear himself away from work long enough to pay her a surprise visit, as he was doing.

Michael had his New York apartment since he was in his early thirties. Its familiarity helped make the at-times long-distance relationship with Sarah, more bearable. She expected to be competing her horses again at jumping shows by late summer, in time for some competitions in Vermont and New Hampshire. Usually Michael let her have her fun and stayed away from the show scene, but this year he would make an appearance. He might even stay overnight. Hopefully the regular nanny for their daughter, Stella, would be back by then. The fill-in was afraid of horses, dogs . . . life?

Michael had to laugh at his joke, but he wasn't making fun of the woman; he wasn't much into animals, himself. Sarah was referred to the fill-in nanny by none other than the regular nanny, Sheila. The latter was supposedly friends with the former. Obviously the pay was the enticement, given how Sarah had declared a substitute nanny should be paid in cash. Michael didn't bother telling her that was going to mess them up at tax time because he wasn't about to lie to the IRS.

Rather than call Sarah, Michael decided the surprise would be even better if he just drove up to the house in his black Chevrolet Impala rental, making Sarah wonder who the heck it was. The paved driveway was a couple-hundred yards long and winding, so he didn't see the house and the car parked to the right of it until he was close. That vehicle was probably the temp help, so he went ahead and parked behind it. Sarah's Range Rover was nowhere to be seen, so it was probably in the garage. When she was staying down here she spent most of her time at the farm, even doing some of the seemingly interminable yard maintenance. The bill for last year alone was something like ten grand. He'd remind her Kentucky had a longer growing season than New York, so maybe the Lexington farm needed to be a thing of the past? There was only so long he intended to drop hints: she was throwing money away by owning this place. (Michael could see why Sarah liked it, however.)

Having gotten out of his rental car, Michael was compelled to linger a minute, taking everything in, as he saw this place so infrequently. Then he thought he heard a moan, emanating from the barn. Immediately he feared Sarah was hurt. As it was, she was still recovering from a bad fall from a horse that stopped at a fence—at a competition. She didn't actually fall off the horse the first time it stopped but the third time she attempted to jump the horse over the fence. Why the flip Sarah had to force the issue . . . Then again, she could be as stubborn as that horse. Fortunately she got rid of that one. On the way to the barn, Michael heard the storm door slam behind him. He spun around to see who emerged from the house—but no one was there. This situation compelled him to reveal something: infrequently though he visited this place, IT NEVER FAILED TO CREEP HIM OUT. And Michael liked to think he'd been around and was quite practical. Formerly he'd chalked up his attitude toward this farm to the fact he was a big-city type and simply couldn't relate to this place.

"Sarah? Sarah!" Michael called upon entering the barn, feeling like he was simultaneously walking into a big, black hole, hearing nothing in response. There were some opened windows for the horses to look outside, but thick metal screens covered the openings. Maybe if more light could infiltrate the barn it wouldn't look so dark. But why was it so quiet, other than the moan he might have heard? He was certain, however, he didn't imagine hearing the storm door slam—he didn't think. Not even a horse was stirring. They weren't outside, as Sarah let them out early in the morning and brought them in by noon, even earlier if she was riding one.

Then Michael had an idea: since this visit of his was a surprise, Sarah was probably surprising him in return, by making noises and hiding. How she pulled off the moan in the barn and then the slam of the storm door was a mystery. Their daughter was too young to be in on the game. Was the fill-in nanny in on it? Doubtful. Michael wasn't in the mood for silliness. He just wanted to see his wife and kid.

"Sarah!" Michael yelled this time, his voice sounding like a squeak. O.K., he admitted it: he was scared. Since his wife wasn't answering, he was going to show her how uninterested he was in playing games and head back to the airport. She'd call him later and pretend he was never here. He'd do the same thing—to save face!

Who would have thought a quick jaunt to Georgetown would turn into an unwanted adventure? Sarah's initial mistake had been to let herself be distracted by the fact "the new nanny" was back at the farm with Stella, and this would be the young woman's first "test." Sarah's daughter could be a real handful—not so much by what she did but what she didn't. In other words, she could be very sneaky, but it was done in all innocence since she was so young. She wasn't yet old enough to be any sort of "threat." However, she did like to go in the barn because she wasn't supposed to on her own. She wasn't (yet) tall enough to open the stall door latches, and Sarah locked Bear in a stall when she went out. Only occasionally had Sarah ever let Stella go in the barn with her, but "the current nanny" was expected to escort her. Fortunately Stella was a bright kid, so when she was four, she would be allowed in the barn, as it shouldn't be necessary to have a nanny watching her every second. Nonetheless, Sarah would still want the nanny to keep an eye on Stella while Sarah was busy with her horses, even if she was just brushing them. Sheila didn't seem to mind the barn, but this temp nanny definitely appeared to have issues. Then again, ever since something at the Lexington farm traumatized Sheila . . . Anyway, Sarah had called the new/temporary nanny, Allison, while driving away from the farm and warned her not to let Stella go to the barn, despite the girl's protests. (Sarah hadn't worded it quite that way.) Then Allison lost track of Stella and that was the last news Sarah had of the situation at home. About two minutes later she was pulling into the supermarket parking lot, completely losing it but trying not to. The last thing Sarah intended to do was hurry back home. Stella loved to try to get Mommy's attention because she never got enough of it! Sarah didn't blame her; she too was often ignored as a kid and was desperate for her mother's attention. It wasn't too difficult because her mother had few interests. Sarah was admittedly obsessed with horses, so the best place to find her was in the barn, whether she was in Conneticut or Kentucky—unless she was at a show. Hopefully Stella would become as obsessed with horses as her mother was.

Just as Sarah parked her Range Rover, her phone rang again. She kept the vehicle in gear while taking the call: it was none other than Sheila Cross, the nanny Allison had temporarily replaced. The former had in fact recommended the latter, and they were supposedly friends. How close they actually were was anyone's guess, and Sarah didn't mind Sheila doing her friend a favor by recommending Allison for this twelve-week term. There were no greetings exchanged, as Sheila launched right into asking, "Have you spoken to Allison lately, Misses Coaten? I called her six or seven times and she won't answer her phone."

"I just got off the phone with her, Sheila," Sarah said, trying to remain calm - or sound calm. She wanted to add something about Stella seemingly having already disappeared under her friend's supervision but held off.

"Oh, O.K.," Sheila said, ready to end the call, aware possibly she was overreacting.

"Everything all right with you? How's your mother?" Sarah asked. She really liked Sheila and wished she hadn't taken a hiatus. Sometimes she wondered if Sheila's mother was actually in a car accident or maybe Sheila just used an accident her mother had, to bow out of coming back here for twelve weeks. As mentioned, something freaked Sheila out the first and last time she was here. She'd tried to hide it but Sarah wasn't fooled.

"She's doing better every day," Sheila replied. "I hope to be able to work for you again when you come back up here."

Sarah told Sheila she hoped as much too and the two exchanged good-byes. Completely distracted, Sarah proceeded to exit her vehicle, neglecting to put it in "Park." Fortunately the parking lot was completely level, or the vehicle would have started moving faster than it did. Sarah never even paid attention as to whether there was a car or truck parked facing her SUV. Stopping her Range Rover suddenly her top priority, Sarah reacted as if the thing was about to go over a cliff. Instead it bumped into a ragged-looking, black Honda Civic—not hard because Sarah stopped the vehicle in time.

Only momentarily could Sarah be proud of how quickly she'd reacted, as the owner of the Civic happened to be in it and leaped out, screaming, "What the # * % @ are you doing, hitting my car?"

Sarah immediately turned off the ignition and got out of her SUV, wanting to see the damage she must have done to the guy's car, even though he hadn't even looked at it. He'd been texting or something and she'd surprised him. He was now flapping his arms and had yet to look at the damage Sarah's Range Rover (hadn't) done to his Civic. It was safe to say he was expecting a payout.

One glance at the front of her Range Rover and foul-mouthed psycho's Civic, and Sarah surmised she'd indeed done a good job of stopping her potentially runaway vehicle. Nonetheless, she'd humor the guy for a minute, continue to let him vent about how badly she supposedly wrecked his car. She was even willing to give him a couple hundred bucks, tell him to get the scuff marks buffed at a body shop and maybe have the whole car buffed while he was at it.

It was possible the guy was high on something (and just a psycho when he wasn't on drugs). Sarah was determined not to lose her temper with him. Fortunately she finally got the guy's attention long enough to ask him, "Sir, did you even yet look at the front of your car? As it happens, my vehicle barely did anything to it."

"Yeah I did, bitch," the jerk replied. "I looked it over even before you. You had your head up your ass the whole time."

Suffice to mention it took everything Sarah possessed in self-control, not to attempt to claw this guy's eyes out, she was that angry. Clenching her teeth, she vowed to continue remaining calm and told herself to "call the Law" if she couldn't endure any more of this crap. The worst thing that could happen was an accident report would be written up and if the idiot decided to waste his time making a claim, it would mess up her perfect record of having never been in an accident nor ever received a speeding ticket.

So far, no one else appeared to be in the parking lot—not a single customer coming or going. A little unsolicited intervention would have been welcomed right about this point in time. One problem was they were in a rather remote part of the huge parking lot. Sarah always parked far away from any store she shopped at because she didn't want any dings on her SUV, ironically enough. Evidently this guy parked out of the way so he could have some relative privacy. Even though she'd unintentionally interrupted him from whatever he was doing, it wasn't necessary to go off on her!

Sarah stared at the guy for a good two minutes, listening to him complain about what she did to his car. At the end he said, "And I just paid it off last week, so this is not the kind of shit I need."

This was a no-win situation for Sarah, so she gave up and called 9-1-1. Meanwhile, psycho-idiot didn't appear to notice, he was still yammering. Maybe she'd get lucky and the cop would haul the guy away on a drug charge and let her go on her way with a warning.

Stella was just a kid but she knew how to get adults super-upset. Here was a new one: she managed to make her new nanny faint! Allison (the lady's name) walked in the barn and was leaning forward like she was trying to see, and Stella cried, "Woof!" causing Allison to fall face-first on the cobblestone barn aisle way.

Shaken by what had just happened, Stella ran back into

the house, which was when her father briefly showed up and then left again right away. He wasn't driving the car he had at home. That one was black too but was fancier-looking. Stella was afraid to greet him because she felt so guilty for having made the new nanny faint.

Meanwhile, the moan Michael thought he heard in the barn was most likely Allison, as she was coming to from her fainting spell. Amazingly who helped her resume consciousness but the feared dog, Bear! He was in front of Allison, licking her forehead. Once she became aware of what was transpiring, she was no longer afraid.

By the time Allison exited the barn, Michael Coaten was long gone. Who appeared but Stella, looking contrite. Allison told her, "Do not run in here and hide from me ever again, Stella!"

Before Stella could apologize, Bear reappeared and she declared, "Mom always locks him up in a stall before she goes out. He couldn't be loose right now unless you let him out."

Given the way the stall latches were set up, it was impossible Bear opened the stall door himself. Although Stella was precocious, it didn't enable her to open any stall doors because the latches were too high for her to reach. Allison just shook her head in reply to what Stella had said.

Sarah Coaten drove up to the barn just as Allison emerged, holding Stella's hand, Bear walking right behind them.

Expect the Unexpected

My friend Dora was leaving for work one spring morning, and a front seat passenger in her red Jeep Liberty caused me to make her stop. She wasn't dating anyone that I was aware of, so naturally I was curious to see who she must have spent the night with. Completely shameless I was. Dora knew this and had a great sense of humor. Therefore, it wasn't too surprising her "friend" was actually a life-sized, blow-up doll, in the form of a male model! She started laughing hysterically as soon as she stopped for me behind the six-floor apartment building we both lived in, located in Scottsdale, Arizona, she on the first floor, me on the third. I had just taken a bag of garbage out to the dumpster and was still in my pajamas, although I was wearing more sensible footwear than my pink faux-fur slippers.

"That's Ernie," Dora said, finally containing her laughter long enough to disclose as much.

"How'd you come up with that name?" I just had to ask. I already forgot to ask why Ernie was going to work with her. With Dora, expect the unexpected. It was a good reason not to give her a key to my apartment, as she might play a prank on me. However, she had a key so she could take care of my cat Chloe on the rare occasion I went out of town for a day or two, usually to visit my parents, Luke and Susan, in Silver City, New Mexico.

"I combined the first letters of the names of all the boyfriends I ever had!"

In that moment I almost felt sorry for Dora because she

had to go through five relationships before realizing she was lousy at picking men. Her last lover was still married, although he was legally separated. A bigger problem was he happened to be her supervisor at work. He ended up losing his job because of his dalliance and then became a mooch for a year—at Dora's expense. The blow-up Ken doll was making more and more sense, sparing Dora from having to explain herself. I had a terrible track record with men, so I was in no way judging my friend.

Finally I asked Dora the obvious: "Why is he going to work with you?"

"I'm lonely, Brenda!" she replied and waved. It was plain she didn't want to go into detail.

Dora left before I could ask her where she got Ernie. I had to hand it to her, if men could get excited about inflatable female dolls, why couldn't we have our own version? Before I had to report to work, I would go online and see if I could order an inflatable doll of my own. It was possible I would lose interest once I found out the price of one. Dora seemed to have a lot more disposable income than I did, giving her more latitude when it came to purchasing "luxury items." She had more expenses when her dog Billy was still with us, but he passed away two-and-a-half years ago. And that alone was an issue because she was lonely ever since she lost her "best friend" (Dora's own description of her pooch). Shortly thereafter she'd begun "the supervisor affair," a total dead-end, yet she threw herself into the relationship nonetheless. She should have gotten another dog rather than try to "help" the guy.

I went back to my apartment, glad to have Chloe, who didn't have to be walked every morning. Cleaning the litter box wasn't the worst thing. Having made that declaration, no sooner did I enter the door, I spied a blob of throw-up on the five by seven beige twill rug under the dining room table. Chloe had never before thrown up, so of course I was immediately concerned about her, but I was simultaneously furious about what happened to the rug. I could clean it all I wanted and possibly there would be no stain, but I would know: at one point there was throw-up in a certain spot. At least there was only me to complain about it; I hated to be seconded by someone when it involved something I was plenty upset about on my own. The last ex-boyfriend of mine never did like my cat. That was a lot of why we never went the distance. As it was, I could never last any length of time in a relationship because I inevitably became bored. Also, I had no problem being alone/single. Maybe monogamy just wasn't my thing—or marriage, for that matter.

Chloe didn't appear ill, but I would keep an eye on her. Meanwhile I'd look for an inflatable doll online. I hadn't taken a sick day for myself in six years, so I decided I was owed a sick day.

I called my supervisor (I worked at a call center for a major mobile phone company) and told him I couldn't make it to work, only to be asked why not. I figured there'd be some understanding from him when I mentioned my cat possibly being sick and me wanting to keep an eye on her for awhile and possibly taking her to the vet if need be.

"I will fire you if you do not get your # % * & butt here at eight forty-five!"

"Yes sir," I replied. Then I looked over at Chloe (back over on the rug) and she threw up again, twice as much as before.

I cleaned it all up the best I could and then took a shower. Afterward I was so drowsy I could hardly get dressed. Hopefully my cat didn't die while I was at work. As for the inflatable doll? I'd search for the website during one of my breaks. However, it sounded less and less interesting. Only Dora could find a use for one of those. Meanwhile I'd be left staring at it. I sure wouldn't drive to work with it. Obviously my workplace was hardly one that engendered humor and light-heartedness. Dora worked at a call center too—for a credit card company. She hadn't worked there as long as I'd been at my current job and she made more money. Also, her commute took less time, and she had a female supervisor this time around.

Dora's dedication to her deceased dog, Billy, was admirable. She not only took him to the dog park several times a week (it was located at the south end of the apartment complex), she'd walk him every morning. He was as enthused about their busy schedule as she was, so it was a total shock when he became ill seemingly all at once. That made losing him especially hard for Dora because she'd taken him on his last walk one morning, unaware he'd be dead by the same time the next day.

In the aftermath of losing Billy, Dora embarked on a quest to find "The One" (as in husband). Maybe grief caused her to pick a man who was even more awful than all the ones before him. It floored me how Ron would order her around while she was supporting him. Maybe it was a matter of him being a supervisor and he just couldn't let that mindset go. Obviously they were in love, or at least Dora was in love with him.

One last check on Chloe confirmed she didn't throw up a third time, which should have energized me, right? Instead I laid on my bed for a minute, just to "rest." All I could think was, I'd piddled around so much it was possible I'd be a couple minutes late for work, even without laying down before leaving. Mr. Palmer already went off on me once, but it was possible he'd do so again. I despised being yelled at twice for the same thing—especially since he overreacted the first time. Maybe he simply didn't like cats. Or me. I didn't like "not being liked," if only because I tried so hard to be likable.

Usually I took Camelback Road all the way to I-17 South, which crossed I-10. I took that westbound to Goodyear, where I worked in a one-story, non-descript-looking building located in Saguaro Industrial Park. The apartment complex was close to the dividing line between Scottsdale and Phoenix. Barely had I passed the sign that proclaimed "Welcome to Phoenix," when a skinny, long-legged, black and brown dog ran across three lanes of traffic. The two vehicles to my right avoided hitting the mutt, by sheer luck, as the drivers didn't appear to see him. I turned toward the left, where there was a turn lane, but the dog darted right in front of my car and it grazed his left hip. He immediately went down, but I stopped my car before running him over. I turned on the hazard lights and leaped out, my whole body shaking. Fortunately he didn't bother to try and get away from me, as a wave of oncoming vehicles in all three lanes suddenly appeared from the opposite direction of Camelback.

Although the dog had to weigh at least fifty pounds, I proceeded to lift him like he was weighed practically nothing and carried him over to my silver Chevy Sonic, to put him in the back. After opening the hatch and placing him in the car, the look he gave me was absolutely priceless; it was as if he was not only trying to tell me he was grateful, he completely trusted me. I wouldn't have traded that moment for anything, even though doing so was further putting my job in jeopardy.

Meanwhile, not more than a half a mile away, Dora was driving back and forth in front of her ex-boyfriend's house—the one he was sharing with his wife, Kathy, from whom he was still legally separated. He had more feelings for their dog, a Beagle named Chico, than he had for his wife. His favorite pastime was to walk Chico up and down the street where they lived, never venturing far but making several passes, as it were, giving Dora the perfect opportunity to see him. At the same time, she expected Ron to see she had a lover with her. Since it was an inflatable doll, she couldn't let him get too close. It was a shame Dora couldn't get her fill of an unemployed, not-yet-divorced loser, but maybe there was such an undeniable attraction she couldn't help herself.

Finally Ron emerged with Chico, after Dora had driven around the block so many times she'd lost count. It didn't matter to her if she was a little late to work; her new supervisor, Betty, was very understanding. At least she seemed to be. Dora would soon find out for sure.

Dora didn't want to stop and chat with Ron, she just wanted to get his attention and then be on her way (and hopefully he'd see the "second head" in her car as she drove away). She expected to be bombarded with texts and e-mails before she even made it to work. He not only noticed her (mostly because he recognized her red Jeep Liberty), he hurried back into the house, grabbing Chico by the collar, as he wasn't on a leash.

"It really is over," Dora mumbled as she drove west on Lafayette Boulevard, finally heading to her job. If she hadn't taken this slight southbound detour just off Camelback, she would have taken that street all the way to Central Avenue in downtown Phoenix. This route would suffice; for the moment she needed a little change of scenery. Even better, maybe she needed to call in sick at work and go home.

The veterinary clinic I took Chloe to was in the opposite direction of where I was supposed to be driving. Since the dog I'd hit wasn't mine, why didn't I simply drop him off at a vet clinic on Camelback? Truth be told, of all the times I'd commuted to and from work, it was impossible to say I knew where one was. So that was my excuse for deciding to turn around and head to "Scottsdale Veterinary Hospital" on Via Linda, in Scottsdale. Obviously I wasn't worried about what this visit could cost me. In fact I appeared determined to be so late to work I would be certain of losing my job. Maybe Mr. Palmer was a dog-person and would have some sympathy when he heard my story about why I was super-late. (I envisioned showing up at some point on this particular day.)

It was about seven miles to the vet clinic. Stopped at the intersection of Camelback and 68th, I dared to look in the rearview mirror, trying to see what my passenger was doing. I had yet to hear a peep from him, and I didn't know if that was a good thing or not. Admittedly I felt obligated to help the dog, even though it was his owner's fault he was running loose. Although he wasn't wearing a collar he looked too well fed to be a stray. "If things worked out and he became mine," I'd have to move because the apartment complex only allowed one pet. Besides, it would be up to Chloe if the dog could stay, as in she might never get used to him. Worst of all I'd have to get up every morning and take him for a walk—assuming he recovered from his injury.

I was getting way ahead of myself, but I couldn't seem to help it. Then the worst case scenario of all occurred to me: tomorrow morning there would be flyers posted all over the place with the dog's picture and a plea underneath it for whoever finds him to return him. That would really put me in a quandary. One thing was for certain: this dog had suddenly taken over my life.

The veterinary clinic was in an upscale strip mall that had a florist, a womenswear boutique, a gourmet supermarket, etc. Other vet clinics might have been more affordable, if only because they weren't located where the rent was so expensive. I brought Chloe here because a friend of mine from high school, Dr. Becky Smalls, was one of the veterinarians. However, Becky wasn't one of the owners, so it was impossible for her to give me a price break. Under these particular circumstances, it would have really helped.

I didn't park as close to the vet clinic as I would have liked because it was already busy. I considered parking in the fire lane, but I didn't want to make a big deal out of the situation. Then again, I didn't even know this dog, so could I expect him to let me carry him a long distance without him getting upset, possibly even biting me? Besides, given his injury it probably wasn't even advisable for me to carry him very far.

Before going ahead and parking in front of the clinic, I exited my car and checked on the dog, lifting the hatch to have the most unobstructed look.

Nothing. Not even a dog hair. Chloe only came to the vet

once a year, in a crate, so there wasn't even any cat hair back here.

I awoke and sat up so fast it would have been comical—except for the fact I was so % * # @ late for work I was as good as fired. At least I was dressed! Then I looked to my left, where there lay an inflatable male doll. That Dora, expect the unexpected.

Superstitious

"I'm afraid, Mrs. Stranger, Winn Books is not interested in your debut fantasy-romance novel, 'The Magic Mask,'" Editor-in-Chief Joselyn Schmidt told Monty Stranger's widow, Thelma. "Therefore, I won't have time to read it." Ms. Schmidt didn't even want to maintain eye contact with this woman because it was plain she wanted a favor, in the form of a big, fat, book contract. She'd come to New York from Sedona, Arizona, specifically to hand-deliver this supposed masterpiece that Joselyn already knew would be a nightmare to edit because not even the title was grammatically correct. It should have been "The Magical Mask." And she only made it into Joselyn's office because her secretary, Marianne, fell for some bull—t Mrs. Stranger told her. That and Marianne was of course all gaga over meeting the widow of a mega best-selling author. Joselyn wouldn't have even been in the office upon Mrs. Stranger's arrival, except her lunch date had to cancel on her at the last minute. She'd just been debating about what to do for lunch, and her stomach was growling like crazy. All in all, it was a lousy time for Thelma Stranger to just show up at Joselyn's Manhattan office. There was a good time to make an appearance: on the weekends when the office was closed!

It couldn't be emphasized enough, without Monty Stranger's huge publishing successes, Winn Books wouldn't have attained its heightened status in the publishing world. Not only that, Monty could have moved on to another, more established publishing house, but he maintained his allegiance to Winn Books until his untimely death at age 64, having fallen over the second-story balcony outside the "writing room" of his residence in Sedona, which he shared with his wife. It was surprising to Joselyn there was no criminal investigation. Then again, supposedly Mrs. Stranger didn't get a cent of her husband's millions, just the house. All his money and any book royalties from the time of his death three months ago on out would go to maintaining all the non-profit animal shelters throughout Arizona. Suffice to mention Monty Stranger was a dog lover—yet he only wrote about them in his fiction and hadn't owned a dog since he was a teenager.

"On second thought, I'll look the manuscript over after lunch and at least give you a brief critique," Joselyn said. "We won't be able to publish it, but I might be able to refer you to a trustworthy self-publishing company. Write down your e-mail address on this piece of paper. You wouldn't mind doing your own publicity, would you?"

Mrs. Stranger shook her head, as in no, she didn't mind, while writing down her e-mail. She was openly trying to ride the coattails of her deceased husband's publishing successes, the only way she could afford to maintain the 5,000 square foot house he'd willed her. It was better than nothing, considering the fact nearly all his money was "going to the dogs," so to speak. Thelma didn't take it personally. Fortunately Monty also deigned to name her the beneficiary of a (comparatively) small insurance policy. It was possible she wouldn't receive the payout, given the circumstances surrounding his death. It was a freak accident, yet there were probably questions from the insurer's end. Thelma's dilemma was she had no alibi, other than she witnessed his demise. However, when Monty was "in writing mode" (practically all day), he did not want to be disturbed, other than to be delivered a jar of Skippy® peanut butter. He ate it with a silver spoon, which had been the cause of his death because he'd dropped said spoon while admiring the view behind the house while taking a break. Naturally that particular spoon had the utmost significance to him, and he probably feared he'd suffer from writer's block for the rest of his days if he didn't save it. Mere seconds later he was dead, all in the name of an heirloom spoon. Maybe Monty's huge success as a writer made him more eccentric than ever. One thing was for sure: Monty came from nothing and although he made millions with his many bestsellers, all dog-themed fiction, he never failed to be superstitious and a cheapskate whenever the opportunity would present itself! Admittedly Thelma was superstitious, herself.

Joselyn told Mrs. Stranger, "I never did extend my condolences, so I would like to do so at the closing of our meeting and wish you a pleasant stay in New York City. I trust you're not returning immediately to Arizona?"

"I'm staying the night at 'The Honfleur' and flying back home in the morning," Thelma replied. "I'm going to do some sightseeing this afternoon."

"Good for you," Joselyn remarked. "I wish you well."

Thelma could literally feel how deeply this woman sitting opposite her wanted her OUT OF HER OFFICE—FOREVER. All Ms. Schmidt did was give Thelma more incentive than ever to make it in the publishing world. The woman's sudden softening only made Thelma more resolute about becoming a famous writer, with or without Ms. Schmidt's "help."

Joselyn again looked at the title of Thelma Stranger's manuscript and winced. Then she grabbed her cell phone and called her favorite Chinese carry-out restaurant that delivered within fifteen minutes or you received a free item. Afterward she buzzed Marianne and told her lunch was on its way, so let the delivery guy in. Joselyn purposely did not make one effort to ever order anything for her secretary. As soon as you were too nice . . . It was better to be selfish and be done with it. Besides, Marianne angered Joselyn once today, so why reward her?

While waiting for lunch, Joselyn couldn't seem to resist leafing through the first chapter of Thelma Stranger's hokey magic mask nonsense story. Few writers were good at creating interesting titles, including the ultra-successful Monty Stranger. Maybe none of them chose to give it much thought, was all. Someday Joselyn was going to be a writer and quit being a hand-holder, a psychiatrist, and a cheerleader, as well as an exceptional editor. The latter was the only job she truly enjoyed, as being a people-person was a stretch.

Monty Stranger was very talented and creative, although when it came to book titles it was difficult to name one that was brilliant. However, he was forgiven because his short story collections and novels were brilliant and then some. He somehow managed to weave a dog or dogs in all his stories, and Joselyn didn't care a whit about them yet was pulled into everything he wrote. It was safe to say she was in love with the writing of Monty Stranger, may he rest in peace.

Marianne buzzed her boss, Joselyn Schmidt: "Lunch from China House has arrived. The guy brought an extra order of shrimp eggrolls because he's a little late."

"Really?" Joselyn responded, barely able to keep from continuing to read a passage from Thelma Stranger's manuscript. It had to do with a fictitious writer's obsession with Skippy® peanut butter. Joselyn happened to detest peanut butter but was mesmerized by the content – despite the surfeit of grammatical errors.

"Do you want to give me some money to pay for the food?" Marianne asked, starving and irritated with her boss.

"Yes, I'll be right out. And the lunch is yours. I'm busy working on something important," Joselyn replied, hardly able to believe what she just said!

Marianne took the money from her boss and handed it to the delivery guy, including a five-dollar tip. It was surprising her boss was that generous. Even more unbelievable was the fact Marianne just received a free lunch, courtesy of her stingy boss. It was even more notable because Marianne had pissed her off earlier, by letting Monty Stranger's widow in to see her. If only Marianne could write a bestseller, her life would be entirely different. All she needed to do was think of an interesting plot. Her boss deserved credit for accepting writers who didn't have agents. Supposedly none other than Monty Stranger made a name for himself without one. That was pretty inspiring.

Thelma had barely exited the building that housed Winn Books when it occurred to her she probably shouldn't have riddled the manuscript with grammatical errors to help make it appear authentic. She'd thought it would look "strange" if her grammar was as polished as her husband's. As it was, Thelma had been the one who'd typed all of his manuscripts, including editing and proofreading them! Maybe she felt humiliated because of having never been thanked in the beginning or end of even one of his books. Of course Monty did the lions' share involved in creating his masterpieces, but she did her fair share in the background. Full of regret they would not be celebrating their 39th anniversary, Thelma was simultaneously relieved. And she didn't mind the fact his will would allow homeless pets to be provided for better than she would be. If that was what she got for being dutiful, so be it! As it was, being "Mrs. Monty Stranger" had taken its toll because of the boredom involved. He'd always wanted her around the house, to deliver a fresh jar of peanut butter to his writing room if nothing else. It seemed ridiculous to hire someone to do a little thing like that, but looking back, it would have been a good idea. Naturally Monty was far too cheap to have an assistant of any sort, other than his wife. It was regretful she did something that helped cost him his life—not that he wouldn't have leaned over the balcony anyway, to retrieve the spoon he'd carelessly dropped. He should have stayed at his desk to eat the peanut butter. That part was his fault.

Out on the street, Thelma started to wave for a cab (copying what she'd seen others do) and then changed her mind. She proceeded to turn around and walk back into "The Forsythe," the sixteen-story building where Winn Books had its offices. Everything it took to publish a book was undertaken here, save for the binding and printing. Monty had visited many times, as he liked to sign his book contracts in person and chat with everyone. The way he lived at home, Thelma never would have guessed he was capable of socializing for even a few minutes, particularly coming to New York City to do so! He really had lived to write and absolutely nothing more. Anyway, Thelma needed to get her manuscript back before Ms. Schmidt read it. She most likely wouldn't bother, but Thelma would feel better if it was back in her hands. The truth of the matter was the manuscript happened to be copied from a memoir Monty had started and left in a drawer of his beloved writing desk. Thelma had added her own ending (based on facts). She'd also added some supernatural elements to make the story more interesting (and hide the truth within the fiction). You had to read the part she'd added, to find out why that title was appropriate. It was also the number one reason she wanted the manuscript back A.S.A.P., despite flying here to present it to Ms. Schmidt in person. The shock of losing Monty so suddenly must have done this to Thelma, as she was usually a very practical person. However, sometimes she'd get a harebrained idea that seemed perfect at the time . . .

At the sixth floor of The Forsythe, Thelma exited the elevator and directly across the hallway was the door leading to Winn Books' reception area and offices. It appeared to be a sturdy, sound-proof door, yet as soon as she was about to turn the lever she could hear Ms. Schmidt: "I'm telling you, she scared him on purpose and he fell over the balcony 'by accident.' She was wearing a mask. It was probably Halloween evening. I love it. It may be more truth than fiction but it's wonderful!"

Before leaving again, Thelma took a moment to savor the

realization that her writing was impressive enough to excite aloof Ms. Schmidt. It was Thelma's writing too, not just her husband's.

Back out on the street, Thelma was suddenly so overwhelmed by the throngs of people she nearly had a panic attack. As if by instinct, she again waved for a cab and one appeared! Confidently she opened the right rear door and got in. Before the driver even had a chance to ask her where she wanted to go, Thelma stated, " 'The Honfleur', please."

The driver nodded and pulled into traffic, just like that. Thelma was liking her newfound confidence so much she planned on using it, again and again. She might even have publishers in a bidding war over her manuscript. Even better, she might have Ms. Schmidt begging to publish the fictionalized memoir of Monty's life. Winn Books would have Thelma to thank for a change, for its latest bestseller. And no one would have anything on her; Monty fell on his own, plain and simple!

Thelma returned home from the airport in Phoenix via a ride from a limo driver. She'd used the same company Monty did, knowing the rate had to be reasonable. The driver insisted upon carrying Thelma's overnight bag to the front stoop of the two-story log house, although she had already paid him. Then she realized he was probably expecting a tip. A different driver had taken her to the airport and she'd failed to tip him. Therefore, she felt it was necessary to give this guy ten dollars, uncertain if that was even sufficient. He appeared satisfied and fortunately left before she'd unlocked the door. All she wanted right now was to be left alone! Brief though her trip was to New York, everything there was so different from Sedona, she needed some time alone to recover. For once she actually identified with her husband, craving solitude. The house was located on Trailhead Way, offering plenty of privacy yet was only a few blocks from downtown Sedona and overlooked Coconino National Forest. There were two other houses on the cul-de-sac, but both were hidden from view, as they were set further back from the street, each on two acres.

Inside the house, it seemed more quiet than ever. Granted, she'd turned the thermostat up before leaving, so the air conditioner wasn't running. Tonight she'd probably need to turn on the furnace, as there was a March cold snap. Anyway, something seemed different. If nothing else the trip to New York gave her some perspective. As it was, Monty always wanted total quiet. She never even vacuumed until he took a ten-minute walk once or twice a day. Luckily he did that or he would have been severely overweight, given how much peanut butter he consumed—close to a jar, every other day. He didn't like to scrape all of it out of the jar, a rare "indulgence" of his.

Suddenly Thelma was so drawn to her husband's writing room, she couldn't be bothered to unpack her overnight bag. She left it in the foyer and went upstairs, her purse still on her shoulder. Only when she opened the door to the room and the purse fell off her shoulder did she realize it was there. She laughed at how preoccupied she evidently was, not taking seriously the gravity of her mental state. She would have blamed how she felt on jet lag, if only because she was so unused to traveling.

Purse placed on Monty's desk, Thelma made a beeline for the balcony. She just had to see if she could catch even a glimmer of the heirloom spoon, the one Monty had dropped and essentially died for.

Monty always was jealous of how good Thelma's eyesight was, as he wore trifocals. She only needed reading glasses, and her vison for distance was still 20/20. At least she'd had something on him, since she would never be the writing success he was, given her late start. However, she was up for the challenge. So where was that spoon he'd dropped?

Found

"How much is that doggie in the window?" Nan said as she looked at a dog in the pet department of "Pets and Patios" in Chaltham, Indiana, recalling a line from a song she'd heard as a child. She was just joking and needed some comic relief. Formerly the huge store only sold puppies from breeders, but the ongoing outcry about alleged "puppy mills" had compelled the owner of the store to switch to offering dogs and cats for adoption. That killed a lot of profit generated from sales of purebred puppies, but Mel Morgan, the owner, didn't feel he had any choice. There was more foot traffic than ever thanks to having dogs available for adoption, versus cute but high-priced purebred puppies. He had to hope the customers spent money on other items, including pet products. The dog Nan had her eye on wasn't cute in the traditional sense; he was quite an ugly Rottweiler mix. He was five- years-old, according to what was written on the index card in the top right hand corner of his cage. At least he deigned to slightly acknowledge her, which many of these rescue dogs didn't do. She could hardly keep from crying because she'd think they were too depressed to look at her. Was she giving them too much credit? She was a horse person first and foremost and hadn't owned a dog for easily ten years, although it didn't seem like it could have been that long. Her point of reference was when her husband, Jared, was killed in a riding accident a decade ago. He never cared much for dogs, even to have one around the barn, so she never bothered to get another one, having lost "Amigo" shortly before meeting Jared.

Anyway, the dog she was staring at while talking to herself looked very similar to Amigo, who was her best friend (until her husband came along) and was a Rottweiler mix too. He wasn't exactly cute either but was so loyal! She still cried from time to time, thinking about him. She still occasionally "lost it" when she thought about Jared, but he'd caused the accident that killed him by making the horse he was training, rear, expecting to cure the animal from a dangerous habit.

Finally the dog, whose name was "Jester," really looked at her but didn't appear depressed. If anything he looked expectant and wanted to meet her. She decided to keep standing here another minute or two before attempting to bond with him. Her biggest fear was she'd like him but he would be uninterested in her. She was lonely and needed a companion right away and didn't even want a puppy at this point in her life. She'd tried the dating scene but compared everyone to Jared. The fact they'd had so little time together made her more critical than ever of other men. Besides, few of them were into horses, so it became a waste of time to date a guy who wasn't. She used to show quite extensively on the hunter-jumper circuit, which would have enabled her to meet someone like-minded. These days she boarded a few horses and gave lessons, nothing like when Jared was here. Then, there was a waiting list for boarding, training and lessons. The twenty-acre property was manageable on her own, so Nan was able to continue without him, using a contractor or handyman for this or that. It helped to stay busy; otherwise there would be time to feel sorry for herself. Besides, she ran the place for years before Jared came along, having long ago resigned herself to "going it alone."

Ben felt totally rotten, inside and out. If it was possible to physically rot while still living and breathing while appearing normal to everyone else, then that was happening to him. His wife, Helene, took their two kids, Dwight and Diane, to her parents' five-acre estate in Barrington, Illinois, over a month ago, and it was looking like she wasn't bringing them home. She basically went back to "the money," which her family had plenty of. However, by marrying him, she'd essentially given all of it up because her parents didn't like him and in turn supposedly disinherited her. It didn't help Ben had lost his job as a cabinet maker and just recently got a new and better-paying job (but he still made cabinets). It wasn't like he was going to lose the house, so Helene's reason for leaving had to do with her parents having worn her down. The kids would be starting school again in another month, so she'd have to decide where they would be living. (She'd never home-school them.) One bright side was Helene let him talk to the kids on the phone every night. It was better than nothing. He just hoped she didn't tell them he kicked them out of the house or some other lie. Anything was possible. Helene and he'd married and had two kids without really knowing one another. Both had confessed to falling in love at first sight, and she must have fallen out of love with him just as quickly. Ben's new boss had told him he needed to get a lawyer, but it was impossible for him to even consider it. In the meantime he pretended Helene had taken the kids to her parents' for an extended summer vacation and would be home in time for them to start school in the fall.

What got to Ben the most was he didn't do anything to deserve this! It just so happened Helene had a career too, as a real estate agent. She'd been having a hard time getting established until a veteran agent at the office where she worked, took her under her wing (took pity on her). Ben had no idea what Helene told the woman, as to why it was suddenly necessary to leave for a month and counting. Meanwhile, Helene did her real estate-related work online and the co-agent, Shelly, did all the running around. It was ironic, how Ben was expected to be patient with his wife making money at a career, yet he lost his job because the owner of the business went bankrupt, making Ben a pariah.

It would have been convenient to blame Shelly for Helene's sudden attitude shift, but the woman was married with two kids, herself. However, they were already in high school. Maybe Shelly once considered up and leaving her husband because things weren't perfect. If that was the case, he wished she'd talk some sense into Helene.

Now for a confession: Ben ended up dumping the family dog at "Pets and Patios," in Chaltham, Indiana, only a few miles from where he lived. They started offering dogs (and cats) for adoption, which also meant they took in unwanted dogs (but only during certain hours). Once it appeared Helene wasn't coming home anytime soon, Ben figured there was no reason to keep the dog around, although Ben was the only one who took care of "Jester," a Rottweiler mix. Initially Helene was enthused about having a dog to help make use of the fenced backyard, but the animal might as well have been a lawn ornament when he was out there. The kids weren't interested in the dog, either. Maybe they were still too young to appreciate having a pet. It was possible the dog wasn't cute enough, but he had a heart of gold.

Right at this moment Ben was about to enter none other than Pets and Patios, first and foremost to check on Jester. Perhaps he was already adopted, although he doubted it. Given his age (five) and relative homeliness, it was possible no one would ever want him. If the dog acknowledged Ben, he intended to reclaim him—provided he could. He never read the fine print of the papers "Judy" from Pets and Patios, had him sign. He couldn't have read it at the time anyway; there were tears in his eyes.

Approaching the pet section, Ben could see there were a few people looking at the dogs and cats. A woman in jeans and a red T-shirt appeared to be stuck in one place. Hopefully she was considering taking Jester home with her.

Indeed, the woman was watching Jester, hoping she got a sign from the dog, as in maybe he'd wink or wave at her? Ben couldn't help thinking that because he desperately needed some comic relief. He continued to hang back, pretending to be picking out some dog treats from a nearby wall display.

Jester must have done something to encourage the woman because she suddenly stepped forward and tapped the glass on the front of his cage, saying, “I see you too buddy!”

Then someone other than Judy, the one who’d taken care of “the surrender of Jester,” appeared from behind the glass cages and asked the woman, “Would you like to see him?”

“I don’t know,” the woman replied.

Ben couldn’t stand it. If she didn’t at least give Jester a chance he might have to step forward and tell her to, which was absolutely ridiculous. It was time for some quick-thinking.

Bumping into the woman, Ben said, “Uh, sorry, ma’am. I was trying to get a better look at that dog named Jester.” Then he pointed at Jester for emphasis.

In the meantime the woman looked around, indicating her disbelief he accidentally bumped into her. However, she didn’t bother saying anything. Ben considered that a sort of success. He decided to forge ahead and told her, “Jester was my dog and I had to put him up for adoption, for too many reasons to list.” Completely involuntarily he started to cry! It would help his cause at least, wouldn’t it?

Jester had yet to take any interest in Ben, but the dog was definitely interested in the woman. That alone should have compelled her to give Jester a few minutes of her time and get to know him. Instead of at least continuing to stand there for another minute, the woman gave Ben a dirty look and left, not even giving Jester one last glance. Ben wanted to exclaim, “I adopted Jester four years ago, myself. Please don’t make the second time around for him, any more miserable than the bare minimum.” At that time, there was a one-day adoption event hosted by Wynne County Animal Shelter, in the parking lot of “Baylor’s,” a supermarket that happened to be a mere few hundred yards from Pets and Patios.

***

Helene Paulson left her husband because she didn't love him anymore. It was impossible to feel guilty, but she was very stressed because at some point it would be necessary to make their break-up permanent (as in divorce him). The last thing she ever wanted to do was put herself through this, having had two kids with the man. She didn't even want anything monetarily from him; she just wanted to be DONE with him. With no warning (including for herself) Helene had packed her Audi wagon with as many of her and the kids' clothes and belongings that would fit, put the kids in the back seat (thankfully they were beyond the ages of needing car seats) and headed north, to her parents'. Rather than feel she was shirking her responsibility as a wife, she finally felt free again. Evidently it was what "falling out of love" felt like. Already she and the kids had been gone for over a month, but it felt like two minutes. She'd been staying busy, doing real estate-related tasks online. However, it involved properties in Indiana, so if she remained here in Barrington, Illinois, it would be necessary to get her Illinois real estate license.

If Helene hadn't been a Realtor, she never would have met Ben. As it was, she'd recently been taken under the wing of a seasoned broker, Shelly Ames, as Helene had been desperate to find leads. Shelly had let her do an open house for a model home in "Sunrise View" subdivision, on the outskirts of Chaltham. Who walked in that Sunday afternoon but the man who'd made the kitchen cabinets for the house, Ben Paulson. He had stopped by to show off his handiwork to his girlfriend, who happened to be "casually looking" for a house for her parents, who were getting ready to downsize. Ben and his girlfriend were the only ones who showed up at the open house that Sunday in late June, and Helene figured she'd never hear from the couple again. Nonetheless she kept thinking about Ben because they'd exchanged a certain look that made her think he felt like she did.

As it turned out, the girlfriend told her parents about the house, and they not only ended up buying it but using Shelly and Helene to sell their other house. While all this was going on, Ben broke up with his girlfriend and asked Helene out, having had it confirmed (by Helene) she was single. Her last relationship had lasted close to ten years, and she was left wondering where the engagement ring was. She would have waited another ten years if only the loser would have been more committal. All this was no excuse to go out with a guy who made cabinets for a living, but she liked to think she wasn't a snoot (unlike her parents, Jack and Andrea). Determined to prove to the world she wasn't like them, she'd accepted a dinner invitation from him. He at least had the sense to take her to downtown Chicago, or she probably wouldn't have gone on a second date with him.

Since Helene and Ben had "houses" in common, if indirectly, it took her no time at all to convince herself he was the one to marry (besides both admitting to "falling in love at first sight"). Finally she could shut her parents up, as they never ceased to remind her it would be more and more difficult to find a husband once she turned forty. (She was thirty-six at the time.) She never would have had the nerve to tell her parents she would have been happy to have a couple kids with a random guy and never see him again. That sounded awful! The guy she'd spent a decade of her life with hadn't wanted marriage (obviously) nor kids, just a live-in lover.

By marrying Ben following a whirlwind courtship, Helene moved into the house Ben had been slowly renovating. It was on an acre in unincorporated Chaltham, and Helene was impressed with the low price he got it for. It had been for sale by owner and might have gone into foreclosure if Ben hadn't come along. He was able to secure a reasonable loan and was so financially responsible, Helene felt like she couldn't not want to marry him. Nonetheless, her parents weren't especially impressed with her cabinet maker husband, and no matter how "happy" she claimed to be, it did no good. Inevitably anytime she'd visit them at their place in Barrington, she'd go alone. Once she had the kids she'd take them along. Meanwhile, Jack and Andrea made no secret of not wanting to see their son-in-law. Ben would try and have a sense of humor about it, claiming staying home gave him more time to work on "their" house. (The mortgage was in his name only.) Helene used to feel sorry for him until her parents drilled it into her head, she needed to feel sorry for herself, for having married such a loser. She couldn't get over the fact she'd used exactly the same word to describe her last boyfriend, so they had to be onto something.

Here Helene was, having not only listened to her parents, she basically moved back in with them, her two kids in tow. She felt like a forty-four-year-old kid, herself. How could she possibly do anything with herself when she still lived under her parents' rule? Their threat of disinheriting her if she didn't dump her husband had turned her into the very person she never wanted to be.

Once she got her Illinois real estate license, Helene intended to get her own place. As it was, their house (the one she grew up in) was so roomy, it wasn't like she and her kids got in anyone's way. Nonetheless, she'd look around for a good buy on something that was as close to her parents' as possible. Hopefully they'd be so thrilled she was permanently staying put, they'd buy the property (but put it in her name). It was the right thing for them to do, if they truly cared about their only child and her two children.

Jester was gone. Ben was both relieved and anxious, standing in front of the empty cage. There were currently only a few dogs available for adoption and there didn't appear to be any cats or kittens. Maybe it was a positive sign overall, but it made the pet department seem very depressing.

Trying to remain upbeat, Ben was already looking forward to the phone call from his kids in a few hours. Both had conveyed hope they were coming home soon, as their mother told them they were leaving soon. Ben hadn't dared ask her to clarify what they'd said and vowed to continue to be patient. Maybe he was too good at that and it was actually working against him.

Ben turned to leave and saw none other than "the woman he'd purposely bumped into," picking out some dog treats. Rather than bump into her again, he waited for her to finish making her choices. When she turned around and saw him, she appeared anything but happy to see him.

"A pleasant surprise, seeing you here," Ben declared, compelling her to nod. However, it was plain she had no intention of lingering. To her back he was forced to ask, "Could you please at least tell me if you adopted Jester?"

"Yes," she answered.

That was exactly what Ben needed to hear. Nonetheless he wasn't finished bothering this woman who had done him a huge favor. He had to show his thanks, so he asked if he could buy her a cup of coffee at the Starbucks® located in a strip mall on the other side of Pets and Patios' parking lot.

Somehow the woman managed to agree to his invitation, so Ben waited near the register while she paid for her pet-related purchases. Only then did he notice she was wearing wedding and engagement rings. Oh well. He'd already made clear to himself, the brief get-together was a way of saying "thanks" to this woman, who was kind enough to adopt Jester. How could Ben help but like her? And it wasn't impossible to like a woman, at the same time not expecting "something more."

Nan wasn't having an easy time with her new dog, Jester. He wasn't keen on coming to her when she called his name, which irritated her. She'd decided to buy some treats to give him whenever he came when called, so maybe he'd learn faster. A quick trip to Pets and Patios was in order, and who approached her there but Jester's former owner. Nan was initially irritated with the guy but ended up accepting an invitation to have a cup of coffee with him. Typically she was pretty wary, but in this case she was compelled to appease him. Maybe the lonely look in his eyes was what did it. He also happened to be easy on the eyes. Some excuse that was.

What Ben had to tell Nan was out-and-out heartbreaking—if it was true. Supposedly his wife took their two kids to live with her parents in Illinois, "just because." (He didn't go into detail on that issue.) However, he did explain his current situation and the difficulty in waiting to see what his wife was going to do with herself. Meanwhile, their kids were stuck in the middle, yet she didn't seem concerned. It wasn't as if he could report them as kidnapped but felt desperate enough to do so. By the time Ben finished lamenting about his personal situation, Nan wanted to lean over the table and give him a hug.

As Nan was sipping her coffee, Ben proceeded to ask her, "What would your husband think of you having an 'innocent' cup of coffee with me?"

Nan almost sprayed a mouthful of coffee all over the table. This was the last question she'd expected from a relative stranger, but she kind of deserved it, walking around wearing her engagement and wedding rings, in Jared's memory.

What Nan wanted to do was exclaim, "None of your business!" However, she wanted nothing more than to tell Ben the truth. Why not? It wasn't like she'd ever see this guy ever again—unless he kept hanging out at Pets and Patios. Next time she needed dog treats, she'd have to go someplace else.

Helene found the perfect place for her and her two kids. It was only about ten minutes from her parents'. The problem was the rent was a little more than she could afford to spend every month. What happened was she had yet to get her parents on board to buy her a place, despite the fact they were "happy" she'd left her husband, so she'd settled on staying in a rental for six months. They'd thought she had saved a lot of money because Ben took care of the monthly mortgage payment himself, even when he'd been temporarily unemployed. He'd never once asked Helene for financial help and looking back, she realized how much of a man he really was. At this point she was completely ambivalent. Her parents' dislike of him was really their problem, and what difference did it make should her parents disinherit her, if they both lived another twenty years or more?

Shelly Ames called right after Helene had given her kids an afternoon snack and was going to have a look at the rental property. Helene's mother was going to watch the kids while Helene was gone. Barely had Shelly greeted her when she asked Helene when she was coming back to Chaltham.

Helene couldn't immediately reply to Shelly's question because it was so unexpected. Usually Shelly was very understanding with Helene, but that was suddenly not the case. In turn, Helene had an epiphany and sat down at the kitchen table, where her two kids were still seated. Her mother was in the sun room, watching television.

Becoming impatient, Shelly asked Helene, "Are you still there? Is everything all right?"

"No, it's not," Helene replied, ready to cry and feeling like an idiot.

"Tell me everything," Shelly said.

Once Helene started to talk it was impossible to stop, which was a relief. Before she had finished her kids had gone into the other room to sit with Grandma. That was fine with Helene. She might cry yet and preferred to do so "in private."

Ben wasn't trying to be a stalker, but it probably seemed like it whether in regard to Nan Goode or Jester. The issue was his frustration with the current state of his personal life. If he'd been cheating on Helene, it would at least make some sense for her to up and leave with their kids. While waiting for their evening phone call, he was looking at the website

Nan had for her "Goode Stable." He was curious where it was located and couldn't resist writing down her first name and phone number(s), leaving the scrap of paper by his computer. Afterward he almost called her! He'd obviously already forgotten he was waiting for his kids to call. He must have enjoyed himself a little too much earlier today. It turned out Nan was a widow and wore her engagement and wedding rings in her husband's memory. The guy was supposedly quite an equestrian but was killed in a horse riding accident, thanks to recklessness on his part. It was so moving, hearing this woman's story about her ill-fated husband, Ben had wanted to give her a kiss afterward. At the same time he was aware his gesture could be taken the wrong way. And maybe it would indeed lead to something more? He was as morally bankrupt as any other guy!

Why hadn't the kids called yet? It was almost eight, and Helene never failed to have them call by seven-thirty. Afterward they took their baths and got ready for bed. Helene really was a good mother, overall. There was no explaining what had happened between them as a couple. It was a shame there was no one reason they were torn apart. If there was, maybe Ben could better accept what appeared to be the end of their marriage. All he asked was for Helene to tell him why she'd fled!

Ben shut down his computer and decided to call Helene's cell phone, as he was sick of wondering why the kids hadn't called. While he was at it, he was prepared to ask her what the flip was going on in her head. Maybe she'd give him an honest reply if put on the spot.

Helene's phone rang and rang, compelling Ben to become concerned. Finally Helene answered, "Ben?" sounding out of breath.

"Yes, it's me," he replied.

"I'm driving, so I had to pull over before I took your call. I don't want to get a ticket."

"Why are you out driving?"

"I'm coming home with the kids."

"Now?"

"Why not?" Helene wanted to know. "I'd rather get the drive out of the way while I'm inspired."

"Inspired?" Ben had to ask. He also wanted to know, "Are you coming home . . . for good?" He cringed asking the second question because it seemed like his peace of mind depended on her reply.

"Yes," she answered. "And I'm sorry for taking off with basically no warning. I guess I needed some time away to think."

"Everything's O.K. now?"

"I think so."

"Are you inspired about us?" Ben couldn't resist asking. He wasn't trying to be sarcastic, but he was admittedly having a difficult time empathizing with her. Not only that he couldn't quit thinking about Nan Goode!

"I'm having trouble hearing you," Helene told him. "I'll see you in a little while."

Ben shook his head, looking at his phone, useless if his wife didn't care to communicate. She would be no different upon her return with the kids. Was he willing to continue to accept the fact it was "just the way she is"? He was giving himself until she got home, to decide. Let her continue to be the wishy-washy one. If they divorced, he could get his office back and it would no longer be "his and hers" anymore. He only used a laptop, but Helene had a personal computer, monitor and an "oversized" printer (in his opinion, regarding the latter). He'd built a desk to accommodate her computer and other hardware. It was amazing she was able to take off with her laptop and still be able to get all her real estate-related work done. She was welcome to take all her gizmos if she permanently left, but Ben was laying claim to the wrap-around desk he'd carefully (and lovingly) crafted.

Helene and the kids didn't end up coming home until after ten. Ben didn't greet anyone because he had to ask

Helene if there had been a lot of traffic or did she have trouble with her car?

"I had barely left my parents' when you called, and we stopped to get something to eat," she replied. Meanwhile, the kids were wired and ran in the house like two hellions.

Ben wondered what Helene had done to the kids while the three of them were away, and he made a joke about as much while helping her unpack her station wagon, parked in the garage next to his pickup truck. Barely had the kids disappeared in the house when they came back through the door leading from the garage to the kitchen, demanding to know (in unison) where Jester was.

It was surprising Dwight and Diane had even noticed the dog was gone. Their reaction to his absence made it impossible for Ben to simply tell them the truth. He had to embellish it so they wouldn't become hysterical. Also, if he gave the "wrong" reply, Helene might get mad at him for "unnecessarily upsetting the kids" and leave again—with or without them, depending on her state of mind. The kids must have been really bored while they were away, and although they didn't mention missing their father, they seemed very happy to be home. Ben wouldn't dare point as much out and hopefully Helene would notice the obvious.

Being kids, Dwight and Diane fortunately didn't remain revved up for long. Besides, it was way past their bedtime. They even toned down their concern about Jester and helped carry some of their possessions in the house, using their pent-up energy. Ben had told Helene about putting Jester up for adoption but never mentioned a word about being obsessed with the whole thing. As for Nan Goode, there was nothing to say about her, other than he appreciated the fact she'd adopted Jester. He certainly didn't tell Helene about her.

Anyway, Helene had told Ben she wasn't going to say anything to the kids about Jester being gone. The way she'd sounded (over the phone) when declaring as much, had compelled Ben to think she wasn't planning on coming home. That was still no excuse for him being unprepared to explain Jester's whereabouts.

Helene came to the rescue and told Dwight and Diane, Jester had gone to live somewhere else, and he was very happy. Meanwhile, Ben had taken a large suitcase of Helene's in the house. They both looked solemn afterward, but at least the subject could be put to rest.

Ben proceeded to indulge in getting a good look at Helene while she was putting together several loose items to take in the house. Although he still loved her, he honestly could not imagine ever again making love to her. It'd been a long time as it was, and neither one of them had ever cheated, at least he never did. Nonetheless, he was willing to "go the distance" with her, despite the fact she had killed his trust. That was an amazing accomplishment on her part, but at least he'd made a decision on the matter.

Helene was actually "happy" to be back home with her husband, and it was impossible to deny the fact their kids were not only happy but relieved, as well. Although they liked their grandparents', there wasn't enough for them to do. They might have even been the ones to wear out the welcome for the three of them. In turn, Helene had to change some plans, having originally intended to remain in Barrington.

It was surprising Dwight and Diane immediately noticed Jester was missing upon their return, but leave it to kids to be aware of just what you think they couldn't care less about. Helene was able to smooth things over with them pretty quickly, helped by the fact Ben had already told her what he'd done with the dog.

The following morning, Ben's parents, Will and Janice, stopped by. Although they lived only a few miles away, they never had much to do with their grandkids. Both had had health issues in the past few years, so it was certainly an understandable situation. However, there was something about the timing of their unannounced visit that really got under Helene's skin. She'd been dusting in the living room when their silver Lexus sedan came up the black-topped driveway. It had to be Will because no one else would drive that slow. And he'd never let his wife drive his car. Albeit good-naturedly Helene declared the following: the senior Mr. Paulson was a male chauvinist pig.

Gritting her teeth, Helene went to the front door. She wanted to open it before he rang the doorbell. That would compel the kids to come running from the basement, where they were occupied with playing ping-pong—or trying to. If their father was home, he'd run down there and try to give them some pointers. He was at work, however, and Helene preferred to leave them alone. At least they temporarily shut up about getting another dog. When they were old enough to play a serious game of ping-pong, maybe the idea of getting another dog would be revisited. As it was, right now it seemed like there was so much to do, not the least of which was Helene needing to get back in her husband's good graces (win back his trust). Ironically, she never cheated on him! Last night she'd wanted him, but he kept his back to her the whole time. He never slept like that. It was tempting to not even try and get close to him again, as she had very little patience. It was amazing she had any with her kids. Obviously she was made to be a mom, although the responsibility wore thin at times.

Ben hated to drag his parents into his personal life, but he'd decided there was no choice. Both of them weren't in the best of health, and that was actually Ben's impetus. Neither one had a whole lot of interaction with their two grandchildren, as they constantly seemed to be off to one doctor's appointment or another and had no time for socializing, at least not with family. There was no better time than right now to basically call them on it—and invite them over. The thing was, he was at work, so if they didn't mind, maybe they could take their grandkids out to lunch? Ben's mother, Janice, thought it was a great idea, but Ben's father, Will, didn't want to impose. If only Ben's father knew the extent of what Helene had done, he wouldn't have hesitated. Fortunately the elder Paulson didn't need too much convincing. That was good because Ben had to get back to work. He was busy filling an order for the gourmet kitchen in a 5,000 square foot house on nearby 600-acre Glass Lake.

Meanwhile, Ben anticipated a phone call from Helene, complaining about his parents' unexpected visit. If she really wanted to knock herself out, she could make lunch for the five of them. However, he was willing to bet she gladly sent the kids off with their "other" grandparents.

By the time Ben took a break and had a sack lunch (he'd prepared it himself, having already gotten used to doing so), there was still no call from Helene, which was concerning. "No news is good news" didn't hold true in regard to his wife. She was always looking for an excuse to go off the deep end on something and couldn't wait around for an explanation. She'd toned it down after having the kids, but it seemed like she was working herself back into the habit. Ben referred to it as a habit because he felt like she could control herself—if she would so choose. Maybe he was being callous, but at this point he didn't care. Nonetheless he still wished she'd call, even to yell at him!

What was this? Helene wondered as much while dusting in the home office for herself and Ben. There was a scrap of paper tucked under his laptop. He rarely used it, which she'd decided was a good thing. She never wanted to be the wife who wondered why her husband seemed to be obsessed with "something online." At least with the kids off to lunch with their "other" grandparents, Helene had an opportunity to do plenty of thinking and snooping, as it turned out. What was written on the other side of the "scrap of paper" but two phone numbers for a woman by the name of Nan.

All Helene had to say to that was good riddance to Ben. He was welcome to her—and the kids, too.

No Real Surprises

I needed a part-time job for supplemental income because my "main job" didn't pay enough. If I had a rich husband like my sister, Emily, did, there wouldn't be an issue. I wasn't complaining, however. She gave me a dog she had bred, a beautiful Yorkshire terrier I named Tilly. I never could have afforded her myself because she was technically a show dog. Emily was a fixture on the dog show circuit, and she was well-known in that circle. There was even a waiting list for the puppies she bred. I found that so admirable I was almost envious. I should have wondered about the repercussions of having such an expensive animal for a pet—and I didn't have her spayed.

If I could have lived my post-high school life over, I would have skipped college, like Emily did. I majored in French but had no inclination to do anything with this acquisition of knowledge. My "problem" was being obsessed with horse shows (versus dog shows). Because I couldn't afford to own and board a horse, travel to shows, pay a trainer, etc., I did what I considered the second best option and that was be a groom—a traveling one, meaning I had the first part of the week free, which was why I took this job at "Woof's," a specialty store for dog food, supplies, and toys. It wasn't the kind of store that could thrive just anywhere, considering some brands of dog biscuits were $12.99 a box—a rather small box, at that.

Why didn't I just work full-time as a groom and not bother with a retail job? The latter was a nice change of pace.

Also, I preferred doing all my horse grooming at the shows, versus dealing with the "everyday" atmosphere found at show stables, at least in regard to hunter-jumper ones.

Emily and I both came from "a horse family," as both our parents, Kaleb and Shanna, had a very successful hunter-jumper stable in Scottsdale, Arizona. Unfortunately they didn't plan for the worst, and when illness struck Dad, there wasn't enough money to pay the medical bills. They were forced to sell the stable to a developer and that was the end of everything they'd established. Dad managed to live a few more years in "a reduced state," but their morale was long gone. I never got over the fact two people could work so hard and simultaneously plan so little, ending up with virtually nothing.

What I ultimately took away from their misfortune was there was no point in working too hard. Nonetheless, I remained obsessed with the horse show world. My mother would school students in the warm-up ring at shows with me literally in a backpack on her back. She didn't want me in one of those things that fit around the front because she was busy changing jump poles and I'd be in her way.

Once Emily was born eight years later, our parents were no longer traveling to as many shows. Possibly that was one reason why my sister never took to horses like I did. However, she liked "the show atmosphere"—for dogs.

It was Monday, so I was here behind the register at Woof's. It was also a rainy, late spring day—and rain around here kept people at home. I was bored out of my mind. I couldn't do any shopping for my dog because I couldn't afford it. The owner, Alexis Mart, would never give me even a ten percent discount. That was fine because the $12.99 box of biscuits would still be overpriced.

What I really wanted was to bring Tilly with me to work, but Alexis forbade it. She was extremely meticulous and was in fact allergic to dogs! As it was, she only showed up for a couple minutes every day, mostly to check on inventory.

Saturday was the only day she worked at the store, and it was closed on Sundays.

About eleven my mother called. She did so every couple of days, just to say hello. Sometimes she stopped in, as her apartment was only a few miles away. I don't know how she didn't go insane with boredom, given how busy she was when she and Dad were running their training stable. She didn't even have a dog, claiming it was "too expensive." It seemed more like she preferred being lonely, so I didn't worry about her as much as I used to. Meanwhile, Emily had given up asking her if she wanted a "free" dog, as Mom obviously had made up her mind.

After complaining about the rainy weather, Mom remarked, "I don't know how Alexis makes any money with that store. A day like today you probably won't have more than two customers."

"I don't need to have very many for Alexis to make money, Mom," I told her. "You've been in here. You've seen the prices on some of this stuff."

"I guess you're right. I may be in there in a few minutes. I need to get out of the apartment for a little bit, and I'd like to see you."

"Stop in, Mom," I said. "I'd like to see you, too."

Waiting for my mother to show up, I walked in circles around the front of the store. Luckily there were no security cameras (I didn't think) because Alexis would have a good laugh. I was laughing at how silly I was being—and didn't care. There wasn't a soul in here, so what was the harm? Alexis Mart didn't have to worry about making a lot of money at this store because her husband, Bernard, was a very successful real estate developer, and her brother, Luke, owned the ten-store strip mall in which Woof's was located. It was entirely possible her rent was no more than a dollar a year. She formerly competed on the hunter-jumper circuit when she was a junior rider, and she had a string of very pricey horses. Her trainer moved to California a couple years ago, after some questionable business practices (falsely claiming some horses she sold were "bombproof"). However, these horses were hardly broke, causing the new owners to fall off and in one case, there was a life-threatening injury of an owner/rider as a result of the trainer's outright lie.

Before Mom had a chance to show up, Alexis came in the front door, like she was a customer. I couldn't help but think she was checking up on me, not just showing up to take inventory. The latter was understandably an ongoing responsibility for a retail business, but she appeared to be obsessed with it.

Fortunately I had long ago stopped walking in circles right inside the glass entry door.

After Alexis and I exchanged good mornings, she quickly glanced at everything (she was "doing inventory"—she had it down to a science) and asked, "Are you interested in becoming partners with me with this place?"

I was so shocked by her question, it was impossible to immediately reply. Meanwhile, I kept dusting the glass case on the counter by the register. In it, there were dog breed earrings. Alexis was slowly incorporating jewelry and accessories into her store (all dog-themed, of course), and I agreed it was a great idea. I'd never told her as much, so why did she assume I might want to be her business partner?

Finally I replied, "I appreciate the fact you asked me, but I have absolutely no business acumen."

After a hearty laugh, Alexis said, "You couldn't have stated the reason any better. You're just wary, is all. Wouldn't you like knowing you have an honest-to-goodness investment in something?"

I hated to disappoint her, but it was time for Alexis to know I wasn't wealthy or she'd keep bringing up the subject. I took a couple seconds to think about how to tell her as much, and the store's phone rang. "I'll get it," she said and disappeared in the back, avoiding using the phone by the register. What was up with that? Since she'd walked in here clutching her cell phone, it should have been the source of any clandestine calls. Then again, she was married, and . . .

I continued dusting the glass case, including inside, expecting Alexis to return soon. Apparently I couldn't move on to another task. After a couple minutes, the first customer of the day still hadn't shown up, but my mother made an appearance. In the meantime, Alexis hadn't emerged from the back of the store.

My mother physically looked nothing like she formerly did. Not only did she lose the love of her life, she had no life! It was impossible not to keep harping on as much, and her changed appearance was proof she desperately needed company and something to do. Taking care of a dog would be a great remedy.

We hugged and Mom then looked around, saying, "The store is finally looking more crowded with merchandise. Is Alexis selling more or having more trouble getting rid of it?"

I laughed at Mom's joke and told her, "No one's been in here yet today, but business has been pretty good overall, at least when I've been here." I almost mentioned something about Alexis' proposition I become her business partner with this store, but my mother would be the one laughing next. She wasn't a mean-spirited person, but occasionally she could be insensitive. Emily resented that about her, and after having made her repeated offers to Mom for a "free dog," had little contact with her. Those two were never close, so it wasn't a surprise. Actually, Emily and I weren't close, either. One reason was we had very little in common. Also, she was on the road a lot, going to dog shows, which left her little free time. Her husband, Hugh, joined her when he could, but he had zero interest in the dog show atmosphere. Their marriage was already at the seven-year mark, so they were either respectful of giving each other space or were on the verge of a permanent separation. It would be impossible for her to match what our parents had in their union; they were in love until the very end. If Dad were still here, he and Mom would have been together, even if it meant sharing a cramped apartment. Emily had a tendency to become tired of anyone who became too familiar. Hugh would probably become a casualty at some point. As it was, Emily enjoyed being sneaky, just to see what she could get by with. We were polar opposites in that regard. Therefore, it was impossible to guess what crazy idea she might have.

Mom and I had been chatting about the weather and this and that. Meanwhile, Alexis continued to remain in the back of the store. I finally couldn't resist telling her about Alexis showing up and then running in the back to answer the ringing phone.

"Is that Alexis' silver Lamborghini out front?" Mom asked.

"Maybe. She and Bernard have several vehicles," I replied. "I don't know what she drives here. Usually she parks in the back and enters that way but not today."

"Do you think her husband is in the car, keeping an eye on her?"

"How would I know? You just walked past the car! Was he sitting in the driver's seat?"

"The windows were so darkly-tinted, I couldn't tell, not that I was really looking."

Suddenly it occurred to me, Alexis could have finished her phone call and was eavesdropping on us, so I whispered, "Maybe we shouldn't speculate about all this right here." Even though I didn't care to be a business partner of Alexis', I certainly didn't want to be fired.

"What are you doing this evening?" Mom wanted to know.

"Laundry," I replied, not trying to be funny. I had a tendency to leave dirty clothes in a pile until there was literally nothing left to wear. "How about yourself?"

"I had a neighbor who lives in the pet-friendly building next to mine, ask me out to dinner. I've seen him out and about but never with a dog."

"Wonderful!" I told her. Finally someone was going to save my mother from having to spend yet another evening alone. If having a dog was out of the question, a man would do.

"I haven't accepted the invite yet," she said. "I'm going to use you as an excuse if I decide to tell him 'no.' I'm going to say you're under the weather and I have to pay you a visit, instead of going out. Since I know you'll be home, I can go ahead with my idea."

I shook my head the whole time Mom was talking. What was wrong with going out with the guy? She never was one to make a big deal out of anything and had expected her two daughters to be the same way. Naturally she didn't get any sympathy from me! I wanted to scream at her to just go out with the man, but I held my tongue.

Mom and I exchanged good-byes and I saw her to the door—so I could ascertain if the Lamborghini was still parked in front, which it wasn't. There went investigating if Mr. Bernard Mart, Alexis' husband, was in it.

Rather than say one last good-bye, I told my mother, "Please go out with the dog-man, Mom. Do it for me, if nothing else."

She did a double-take, as if unable to believe I could be so pushy about going out with a neighbor who was essentially a complete stranger. Then she said, "All right, I will."

No sooner had I turned around and Alexis was behind me, exclaiming, "There you are! Were you about to go outside for a smoke?"

"I don't smoke," I told her. "You know that."

"People change and pick up all kinds of habits, good and bad."

I wanted to tell her I had enough of the latter, but I felt inferior to her. It had nothing to do with the fact she was well-off. It was her height. She was close to six feet tall (versus my five-foot-five). Not only that, she always wore high-heels—and she could evidently sprint in them.

What I did tell her was, "My mom stopped by for a couple minutes and I was seeing her out the door."

"Sorry I missed her," Alexis said. "Did you tell her about my 'proposition'?"

"No, I didn't," I replied. "I couldn't afford to be your business partner anyway. I know you were at the shows in my parents' heyday, so it probably seemed like we had a lot of money, but when my dad became ill, that was the end of the stable and their comfortable lifestyle. I never had it as good myself, once I was on my own, but I'm not complaining."

"Oh." That was the extent of Alexis' response, which wasn't surprising. I would have even preferred having her say, "Too bad, kiddo" (although we were the same age). "If your parents had been crooked, like my trainer, Teresa Sykes, they could have stockpiled some serious cash. Word around the shows was they were honest folks."

I began rearranging the "dog rainwear" that was on a metal rack to the right of the entrance. Maybe one of these would be sold today, although it was supposed to be sunny later. Meanwhile, Alexis said, "Have a great week if I don't see you. You're still Monday to Wednesday, right?"

"This week I'll be in on Thursday from ten 'til twelve because Mandy can't make it in until noon." Mandy Rollins was the other employee of Alexis'. "Then I'm off to West World." That was Scottsdale's mega-center for horse shows and other functions. I would be on a braiding and grooming bender, with Tilly in tow. At least that was one workplace where my dog was welcome.

"I always say I'm going to compete again, and I'm tempted whenever I hear that place mentioned. I hope to stop by there Friday, if I have a minute. I'd tried showing again with my new horse, Limerick, but they were just dinky shows and didn't inspire me. Maybe I don't have enough discipline anymore. Anyway, right now I'm planning a super-secret, super-surprise b-day party for Bernard's sixtieth. I'd told the party planner to call me here at a specific time, so that's why I ran in here and grabbed the call. If it wasn't the planner, I figured I saved you from having to answer the phone. And I'd forgotten my key, so I had to come in the front. It was that or bang on the back door."

I was relieved to hear my boss wasn't having an affair, after all. I obviously held her in high regard. Nonetheless, something continued nagging at me. However, it was none of my business what she did in her personal life. Alexis had yet to invite me to the party, but I didn't expect as much. I'd worked at her store for almost four years but didn't really know her. When competing at the shows, she was one of those who only saw her mounts ringside—to ride in the class. Afterward she'd dismount and go sit in the stands or socialize. Nowadays she boarded at Ann Welder's "Tomahawk Trail Riding Stable." Ann mostly went to "dinky" shows, and when my boss Cindy went to those, she only took a couple riders and a groom or two, including Ramiro.

This weekend, I planned on making some decent money, as I was not only grooming for "Green Briar Stable," I intended to braid as many manes as I could, not just for the horses and ponies with Green Briar. Lately I'd been thinking I was "too old" to stand on a step ladder and braid, but the only limitation was me not wanting to do it anymore. At that point in time, I would quit.

The sun had managed to come out by the time I was locking up Woof's for the day. In the meantime, I did in fact sell a cute yellow raincoat to a lady for her white toy poodle, "Figaro." She was my only customer, but the time passed pretty quickly as the day wore on. It helped having her linger and chat for a few minutes. She claimed to have competed on the dog show circuit and knew my sister "in her early years." Then she added, "She was always something else, a real livewire." Afterward she winked! I had no idea what she was inferring.

I got home and faced the pile of laundry I had waiting for me. I asked myself when the last time was, I went on a date? That sounded more appealing than doing laundry, and my preferred way to meet someone was going to a favorite bar and hanging out. There were some female acquaintances I would casually meet there from time to time, and we basically kept each other company while hoping a man would show up to "save" us. (Women were hopeless romantics and/or secretly desperate.)

The thing was, I wasn't desperate (or lonely). Not only did I have Tilly, I long ago gave up meeting a guy and falling in love. No one seemed to have the patience for that anymore, me included. I could ask for nothing more than to have Tilly thrilled to see me whenever I came home. Thursday we would be going to the show, so I could tie her close to wherever I was braiding, usually right outside the stall the horse (or pony) was in. Fortunately she never had any inclination to run away, but on occasion I worried someone might steal her if I wasn't super-vigilant.

Sitting on the floor, I petted Tilly, the washing machine running. This was utter peace. Then Mandy Rollins called. We weren't friends per se, but she and I were Alexis' only two employees. Hellos out of the way, she asked me, "Lenore, could you work the whole day, Thursday?"

"Well, I . . ."

Mandy cut in to add, "It's only Monday, so it's not like you're not getting plenty of warning."

"I'm grooming for Cindy at Green Briar, starting Thursday afternoon at West World. She won't be too happy to hear I won't be there to help her riders get ready for their warm-up classes." Having said as much, I felt like a selfish pig. Mandy was a single mom, raising a daughter, Sandra, who had ongoing health issues.

Indeed, Mandy revealed Sandra was having some tests done at the hospital, so it was uncertain if she could make it in to work by noon, having initially thought she could.

I told her I would work the whole day, after all. Cindy Shields, the owner/trainer of Green Briar Stable, would have to be understanding, not one of her strong suits. Nothing was more important than "the horse show world," and she expected everyone else to feel exactly the same way. Of course I did, but I also considered myself relatively conscientious. I would tell Cindy exactly why I couldn't help Thursday afternoon, and she was welcome to fire me if she wanted. Glen Roth at "Cactus Flower Stable" had been pestering me about working for him. He'd want me to quit working at Woof's and not only work for him full-time but travel to shows all over the country. I'd done enough living out of a suitcase as a kid.

I decided to text Cindy right then, letting her know I wouldn't be available to groom at the show until early Friday morning (after all the braiding was finished). I didn't immediately receive a reply, so I figured she was probably busy giving a lesson. That may have been, but when she did finally text me back, she didn't sound pleased: "Why does my most hard-working employee do this to me? Are you hinting you need a raise? Just say so, versus effing with me!"

My reply was: "No, not at all. I have to work extra for Mandy, who's kid is having some tests at the hospital." I figured a word in there somewhere would draw some sympathy out of Cindy.

Instead she replied: "Another dumb b— who takes sympathy from whoever'll give it to her. U R her latest conquest!!"

I replied with: "See you Friday morning!" I almost told her I quit but wasn't quite ready. By the end of the weekend, I fully expected a different attitude from myself. I also had a feeling something very interesting was up, yet I couldn't have even begun to imagine what exactly it might be.

Alexis stopped in Woof's Tuesday and Wednesday, doing her brief once-over after coming in the back door, as she usually did. I'd wanted to ask her how the plans were progressing for her husband's surprise birthday party, but she looked preoccupied.

Meanwhile, my mother called me Tuesday morning on my cell phone, before I'd left for work, to tell me she'd indeed gone out with her neighbor, "Henry Penfield." His dog, "Mercy," had been deceased for two years! No wonder she never saw the guy with his dog. He remained in the pet-friendly apartment building because he had a five-year lease and wanted to get another dog but was "still grieving." I asked if it was a good thing my mother had dinner with him?

"Yes!" she replied. "He's very nice. He even offered to pay for my dinner, but we split the bill." Then she asked, "Are you still going to be at the show Thursday?" Despite being out of the horse show loop, it was still important to her, keeping up with whatever was going on. I told her about my change in plans, to which she added, "I'll see you there Friday, around noon. I'll bring lunch."

Tilly and I arrived at the showgrounds about 3:30 a.m. Friday morning, which was early even for a first braiding day. We didn't have far to walk because the steel barn in which Green Briar Stable was located, was right across from where I'd parked. That meant I had also parked close to my boss' (Cindy's) motor home. Her white Toyota Rav4 was parked facing it, and the plate read "Gidde Up." To its right, there appeared to be the same, silver Lamborghini I'd seen parked in front of Woof's. Having never seen the back of that one, I couldn't confirm if it had the same license plate as this one. Even around here, you didn't see many Lamborghinis. Whoever drove it was sleeping with Cindy, given how close it was parked to the Rav4.

West World's permanent stabling area had probably 1,000 stalls divided between several barn structures. Sometimes a couple of tents were erected to provide a couple hundred more stalls. Granted, not every stall on the grounds was occupied by a horse or pony because each individual stable had at least one tack or feed room.

I had six to braid for Cindy's riders (two were doing their own braiding), and then Tilly and I were off to do twenty more. I expected to be done by 7:30 a.m., when I had to tack up a horse I'd braided earlier, a low/amateur adult hunter owned by Tabitha Little.

On my way back from the twenty I braided I was waylaid by people wanting me to do "last-minute manes." I liked these because I was paid before I even did the job. Thankfully I'd brought along plenty of yarn. I wasn't having much trouble keeping my fingers limber because I was into the task at hand. I had to say no to the last braiding request, or I'd be late tacking up Tabitha's hunter, Stanley (the gray Quarter Horse gelding's stable name).

Once Tilly and I were close to the stabling area for Green Briar, I heard who sounded like Cindy, angrily yelling. It wasn't unheard of her to lose it, but it sounded like she'd gone off the deep end. Hopefully it wasn't directed at Ramiro Gomez, her favorite groom, who she took to any shows where she only needed one helper (such as the occasional "dinky" competition).

It turned out Cindy was carrying on a tirade directed at her boyfriend, Thad Jameson, who had yet to utter a word. When I rounded the turn, she was holding a curry comb and proceeded to whip it right at Thad's head. He ducked in time, only to have the brush hit a bay pony named Barney, who was being held on a lead rope by his owner, Mindy Melkin. She was here early at the show to do her own grooming, instead of getting ready for school. Her mother, Susan, had given her this opportunity as a "reward." Maybe all the riders weren't lazy, after all. Unfortunately at the moment, Mindy appeared to be half-asleep and was unprepared when Barney threw his head up in response to being hit by the curry comb. The blue nylon lead rope slipped out of her right hand, and in typical pony fashion (they all had a devious side) he took off, heading straight for Tilly and me. First, however, the pony had to pass the two quarreling lovers, but they were too busy staring one another down to even react. Besides, Thad wasn't much of a horseman, unless dating horsewomen counted.

I wish I could say I "saved the day" by grabbing Barney's lead rope in time, all the while keeping a hold of Tilly's leash. Actually, I did but no one seemed to think there was anything heroic about my effort—yet I had the rope burns on my right hand to prove as much. Otherwise the pony would have been free to roam the entirety of West World.

Mindy did thank me, however, and retrieved her pony, but it was doubtful she had any idea how badly my hand hurt. It was possible I wouldn't be able to braid tomorrow—at least not as many as I'd braided today.

Here came Mindy's mom, Susan, balancing a yummy-looking pancake breakfast in one hand and a drink holder in the other, containing two orange juices and a coffee. I took particular notice because I was hungry. Tilly was most likely ready for breakfast again, as I'd fed her before we left home but that was already a long time ago. I carried her water bowl everywhere, so at least she always had fresh water.

My mom was still bringing lunch at noon, so I had that to look forward to. As it was, I'd be too excited to notice I was starving. The first showing day was adrenaline-inducing, even for grooms.

Inside one of Green Briar's two tack rooms, I tied Tilly to a handle on a tack trunk that was in a corner. Never before had I worried about someone stealing her while I was grooming, but today I felt differently. Maybe it had to do with the fact Cindy was practically useless insofar as keeping an eye on things, totally unlike her. Obviously she wasn't finished sparring with her boyfriend, although he wasn't even around Green Briar's stabling area. Maybe he went to fetch breakfast. Since Cindy was skinny and hardly ate, it was doubtful the way to her heart was food, but maybe he was up for trying anything. They hadn't been together for long, at least as far as him staying at a show with her. I'd seen him at Green Briar Stable a couple times, having arrived on a motorcycle. Cindy had already dated every available horse trainer, so she was forced to widen her search.

I tacked up Stanley for the first class in the hunter ring, low hunter. However, his owner was nowhere to be seen. If Tabitha didn't show up by eight, I had "orders" to longe her horse. She wasn't aware of this, but Stanley was longed on many occasions at home, before she'd show up for a lesson. Cindy called this "working the horse down," and she sometimes did the longing honors herself. She once ran a horse in circles to the point the animal collapsed from exhaustion. I'd never witnessed her going to such extremes and didn't care to. Something about her attitude toward her boyfriend told me he was the one who was getting it today – unless he wised up and left the show grounds.

Stanley tacked up, Tabitha still hadn't appeared, so I grabbed a longe line and whip and led Stanley to an area east of the barns, designated specifically for longeing horses and ponies. Before we had left the aisle way, Tabitha showed up wearing her breeches and boots, carrying a garment bag and a saddle. Rather than look pleased to see me leading her horse out for some exercise, she appeared angry, asking, "Why are you longeing Stanley?"

I started explaining I "had to," only to have Cindy appear and state, "Lenore knows to longe any horses whose owners aren't here in a timely manner for the first class."

Tabitha rolled her eyes and said, "I just got a freaking speeding ticket because I overslept! Who the hell's in charge here?"

"I am," Cindy replied.

"I mean, who pays the bills?" Tabitha asked and then looked upward to add, "Why am I having to ask this?"

"Cool it."

"No, I don't have to, since I'm obviously paying for shit I don't even want, such as having my horse longed! You've been hiding it from me, even in your billing, calling it 'lesson and show day prep fees.' What a joke. Stanley's fifteen! Isn't that like ninety in people years?"

"Not quite."

"You're so full of it you wouldn't know if a pile hit you square in the face."

"I won't comment on that, other than to tell you to take your horse elsewhere. It can be done right here at the show. I'm sure there's a trainer who has an extra stall."

"You wanting to dump me because of getting called on for being greedy and inhumane is not exactly surprising, Cindy."

"Whatever. I know Glen Roth is looking for customers."

"Who?"

"Glen with Cactus Flower."

"Point me in the right direction," Tabitha said. "I'll leave my stuff in one of the tack rooms and lead Stanley to Glen's. I'll have Glen Whoever you said his last name was, tell one of his grooms to come back for everything. I know I'm not coming back."

"Of course not. It'll be a long walk as it is, hon. He's stabled way at the end."

"To be honest, Cindy, the farther I am from you, the better."

"O.K. if I e-mail you the last bill or do you want it snail mailed?"

"I can't imagine writing you one last check. Shove it up your ass."

I was shocked to hear that last comment uttered from Tabitha, who was usually anything but blunt. It proved Cindy could even get under the skin of otherwise "nice" people. Meanwhile, I had turned Stanley around, and Tabitha put a lead rope on his halter. I then removed the longe line, which had a chain, something I was surprised she didn't make a comment about. Maybe she wasn't paying any attention. I had long ago gotten out of the habit of longeing Stanley with his bridle (even though it offered the most control). Cindy had told me to never make it look like I used anything of Tabitha's when longeing her horse, all part of being secretive about it. Therefore, I was technically in collusion with Cindy, something of which I was not at all proud.

Despite everything I wished Tabitha good luck, and she replied, "Thanks. I'll see you around."

A longe line with a chain as well as a whip in my possession, I happened to notice Cindy's boyfriend, Thad, exiting the tack room in which I'd left Tilly, carrying her. Rather than ask him what he was up to, I walked right up to him and turned the whip vertically, basically pushing it against his throat. Poor Tilly didn't know what to think, while Thad looked surprised as well. I was astounded by my nerve, but my anger was extremely empowering. I forced Thad to back up all the way to the entrance of the tack room from which he'd just emerged.

Thad meekly said, "Hey, I was just going to take her out for you, as a favor."

"Liar!" I yelled. "You intended to steal her. Put her back right where you found her." He actually appeared hesitant to listen, so I added, "Do it now!"

Not surprisingly Cindy finally had to get in on things and asked, "What's going on?"

Unfailingly I had to heed my boss before doing anything else, so I looked away from Thad for a couple seconds to answer, "Thad's trying to steal my dog." And that was what he proceeded to do, ducking under the whip. However, instead of going in the direction of his Lamborghini, he headed for the rings. Beyond them was a road that circled the grounds. I'd dropped the whip but still had the longe line in my hand and wasn't aware. Maybe my subconscious thought I could lasso Thad with it. I followed him and quickly closed the distance.

It wasn't long before Thad reached the roadway, and he waved at an approaching vehicle, which happened to be a white Lexus RX350, a vehicle my sister's husband recently purchased for her. (I followed Emily's doings via Facebook, where she loved to brag.) The driver slowed, and Thad tried to open the front passenger side door. The window was open, so I could distinctly hear the female driver say, "Lemme stop first, Thad! Jesus!"

The familiar voice confirmed my sister was behind the wheel. Why would she have Thad Jameson steal a dog she'd given me? How did those two manage to cross paths? Did her husband, Hugh, have any idea they were "friends," let alone unlucky in love, Cindy?

"Emily?" I asked, causing Thad to whirl around. I decided to go for it and ran at him full-force, hoping to catch Tilly as he was falling into the SUV and either opened the door and left or fell on his face.

I caught my dog in time, and Thad managed to escape—with my sister driving the getaway car. I couldn't believe what I'd just witnessed, but at least I had Tilly back, shaken up though she appeared to be. I placed her on the ground, and we started walking back to the stabling area. I told her, "I don't know if that was a close call or a very un-funny practical joke." I never did get my sister's sense of humor.

Rather than work for Cindy and her Green Briar Stable any longer, I was suddenly compelled to call it quits and go work for Glen at Cactus Flower. Back at Green Briar's temporary stabling, Cindy was nowhere to be seen. Then I heard her yelling, over by her motor home. Tilly and I found her standing by a flatbed tow truck driver, waving her arms and stringing obscenities together. Meanwhile, the guy was trying to show her a piece of paper. Finally she stopped long enough to glance at it and declare, "Fine, take it! Obviously Thad wasn't keeping up with the payments! I only rode in it one lousy time!"

This seemed liked the perfect time to say farewell to Cindy, so I calmly approached her to say, "Hey, Cindy. I'm going to work for Glen."

"Just like that?"

"Why not? After what your boyfriend just put me through, trying to steal my dog . . ."

"He's not my boyfriend at this point, the loser!"

"I'm sorry things . . ."

"Go! Just go!" Cindy said, ready to start crying.

"I'll be around."

"I know you will. You'll still have to braid for some of my customers, at least for this show."

"I could stay if you really need me and leave after . . ."

"Go, will you? Ramiro will have to step up, is all," Cindy said and walked back to the stabling area. "I don't have a boyfriend, that's my biggest worry. Even worse, I can't even think of any prospects!"

Tilly and I returned to the tack room from which she'd been "stolen." Who was in there but Mindy Melkin and her mother, finishing breakfast. I'd intended to grab the few possessions I'd left in here, including Tilly's water bowl. I thought the Melkins had sat by the rings to have breakfast, but they might have been in here the entire time, including when Thad carried out his crime. It wasn't their fault they didn't know to stop him. As it turned out, I had a hard time stopping him, myself.

Mindy's mother, Susan, asked, "Could you please help Mindy saddle Barney for their first class in a little bit? She's never had so much responsibility all at once. I let her skip school just for this experience, but I don't want her to feel overwhelmed. Cindy had told Ramiro and the other groom, whose name I don't know, to leave Mindy be, but that might not be the best thing, after all."

I started to say, "Hey, lady, I'm outta here!" but I couldn't do it. Maybe I'd inherited some of my parents' positive attributes after all, unlike my sister, Emily.

My mother brought lunch at noon, just as she'd promised. I'd called her well before that to tell her where Green Briar was stabled, so she wouldn't have to search for it. However, by the time she arrived, there was nowhere close for her to park. Therefore, she drove to the end of the aisle way and dropped off the wicker picnic basket containing our lunches. I kept an eye on it while she parked her car. Why should I have trusted anyone not to steal it? Maybe I was super-hungry, versus extremely paranoid. As it was, I would have been more than happy if she'd shown up with fast food. She'd wanted to make the effort to show she cared.

Of course Cindy had to appear while I was standing guard by the picnic basket, and she couldn't wait to say, "I know, I know, you were quitting earlier today and are only staying on to help Mindy Melkin, and you're certainly owed a lunch break, but could you saddle Dolores Smith's horse while you're waiting? She wants to hack him around the grounds."

How I wanted to tell Cindy, "You do it. You need to stay busy to keep your mind off how lovelorn you are." Naturally I kept my mouth shut. Since I had Tilly with me, I tied her to a stall bar outside Ms. Smith's horse's stall, which happened to be right inside the doorway. Therefore, I was still able to keep an eye on the picnic basket (and my dog). I couldn't wait to see (and taste) what my mother had prepared. She always was a good cook, which was admirable, considering the fact she was so busy in her "former life." I was imagining she'd prepared tuna sandwiches, deviled eggs, and brownies, for dessert.

"That looks delicious!" Cindy said, which I heard from inside Marko's stall (the stable name of Dolores Smith's gray Holsteiner gelding). I had already thrown the saddle on Marko, and after securing the reins under the stirrups, I emerged from the stall, expecting to see Cindy digging into the picnic basket lunch.

Instead, my mother was holding the basket lid open, displaying everything. She said, "Cindy, you're welcome to join us. I made plenty of everything."

I wanted to scream, "Mom, no! This should be for just you and me! Cindy doesn't eat hardly anything!"

Cindy accepted my mom's invitation. Not only that, she (Cindy) told me to wait for Dolores to appear and give her a leg-up. She was "somewhere around here." Mounting blocks were for riders like Dolores, who were on their own schedule. Cindy had a mounting block here at the show, and it happened to be right outside Green Briar's stabling area, which also meant it was about five feet from the picnic basket I had been guarding.

I watched as Cindy and my mom walked in the direction of some trees, to the right of Cindy's motor home, behind some parked vehicles. If I'd assumed my mother had prepared lunch for us, I was wrong. I'd wanted the "alone time" to tell her Emily had been an accomplice in attempting to steal Tilly. I'd figured my mom would be relieved she hadn't accepted the puppy Emily had tried to give her. That one too, Emily would have probably wanted back. Then again, my mother would have had the dog fixed, which might have changed things.

The more I thought about everything, whatever Emily's "reason" for wanting Tilly back, wasn't something I needed to disclose to our mother. Cindy did me a favor by crashing the picnic lunch. And I was glad not to have been invited to my boss Alexis' "surprise birthday party" for her husband.

Tilly and I took a walk to the concession stand.

All Alone

The problem with Estrella Street, as ritzy as it was, was the fact practically no one living on it was even close to the same age as Claire. Her husband, Drake, was closer to their ages, but he was still "fully-employed" and traveled practically nonstop for his business. This gave Claire plenty of time to wonder exactly what all her neighbors did, as hardly anyone appeared to stir from their 5,000–10,000 square-foot adobe and Mediterranean-style houses. The only exception was a relatively young-looking couple who typically walked their dog every morning around nine. Claire too liked to take a walk every day, but she usually did so about noon, whether or not she'd "slept in" (unless her husband was home). If Drake was around she made sure she got up by eight, to make him breakfast. Otherwise she'd look ungrateful for how well he provided for her.

Married life was good, now that Claire had become accustomed to the fact her husband was away all the time. At first she'd taken it personally and thought perhaps he was cheating on her whenever he'd go on his business trips, but that was impossible if only because he hadn't made her sign a pre-nup. That had to mean he would never give her a good reason to want a divorce. Living in Drake's 7,500 square-foot, Mediterranean-style manse for the past two years, virtually alone, had given Claire plenty of time to wonder what it would be like to eliminate her husband from the picture—not literally, of course. It was pure fantasy to divorce him, but she bet plenty of women divorced because they were lonely, including the ones who had kids.

Being a mom had never been an aspiration of Claire's, but she sometimes wished it had been. That way she would have been more willing to settle for someone to marry, long ago. Tying the knot at forty was fulfilling, but at the same time she'd become accustomed to her autonomy. Obviously she had more financial security than she ever could have realized on her own, but . . . The saddest part of the whole situation was the fact her family started making not-too-subtle requests for financial help the moment Claire and Drake had tied the knot. To think, she was the family member no one had any expectation for realizing financial success. Didn't marrying money, count?

Claire needed to get a dog. The biggest problem? She was too used to doing nothing all day! However, there was always a "family dog" in her life, that she could remember. When she left home at eighteen, finding an affordable place to live and paying the bills comprised her world. Owning a dog was out of the question, not that she wasn't lonely on plenty of occasions through her twenties and thirties. Something about seeing that too good-looking couple walking their dog time and again, stirred something in Claire. They were doing something uncomplicated together. Drake and she had virtually nothing in common, but at the very least they could walk a dog, the rare times he was home. Meanwhile the dog could be her constant companion. She couldn't count on any girlfriends on a regular basis because everyone was tied up with kids and/or jobs.

Indeed, Claire was "living the life." It was amazing she made any effort to stay in shape because she was so lazy. Maybe she kept it in mind, if things didn't work out in her marriage . . . Nonetheless, she really did enjoy her daily walk, even if she usually took it in the afternoon, including in the middle of summer. Sometimes "the couple" would be out then, although they wouldn't have their dog with them. Morning was definitely their favorite time to walk him, but

Claire wasn't always up early enough to know their exact schedule . . . Why were they so important to her, aside from the fact they appeared to be the only couple on the street who stirred from their house? She only knew they were residents because on a few occasions she saw them walk up the driveway of a house on the other side of Estrella, five houses to the west. Given the large lots, that was rather far. It wasn't something Claire could have noticed unless she was really watching them.

If Claire had a dog, she would force herself to take a walk earlier. The late spring and summer heat never bothered her, in part because she was from around here. So was Drake. In fact, he was raised right here in Scottsdale, although he attended college on the East Coast. At first some of the things he would tell her, made her think he was just trying to impress her and wasn't even telling the truth. Then, as she got to know him, she came to realize he was most likely not even revealing as much about his accomplishments as he could have. It wasn't long before Claire had fallen in love with him, yet all she knew about Drake's livelihood was he was an "engineer." It wasn't until they were engaged, Claire admitted she thought he was referring to a train when he'd mentioned being an engineer. He'd heartily laughed. Then he leaned in for a kiss. His timing was infallible. Not only that, he had movie star looks and was very intelligent (duh!), so was it really that important what Drake did for a living, even if it kept him away for long stretches of time? Besides, he had a great sense of humor. Claire never once wondered if he had money or not. In other words, she'd loved him "for him," from the start, and he was aware of as much. He was in fact so perfect he didn't seem real, although he was exactly the kind of man she'd requested dating when signing up with "perfect men and women.com."

This evening around six, Drake was returning from his latest junket. As usual, he was getting a ride back from the airport in a hired limo. He had never mentioned wanting

Claire to pick him up, but she had offered to do so, soon after they were married. In turn he'd sounded annoyed when telling her "no." There were newer, matching, black Mercedes sedans in the three-car garage, so it wasn't like she couldn't pick him up in something classy—not that Drake would have had it any other way.

Anyway, Claire had a surprise for Drake: she bought a puppy! She'd first gone to a couple animal shelters but was told she had to apply for an adoption before she could actually bring the dog home. She had no patience for that sort of thing. No wonder pet shops still thrived.

Claire went to "The Pet Stop," in Roadrunner Crossing, a strip mall in Mesa, and bought a beautiful (but quite furry), ten-week-old, female Sheltie (Shetland Sheepdog). Claire picked the name "Lucy" because she liked it and would have named her daughter that if she'd had kids. The two bonded immediately, which was very reassuring.

Since Claire had zero supplies for a new puppy, it was necessary to purchase "everything," providing a field day for the saleslady helping her. As the purchases were being rung up (after the price of the puppy), all Claire could think about was Drake's shock upon seeing the total on the credit card statement. Long before then, however, Claire expected to smooth things over. In other words, tonight! Admittedly, she had no idea what his opinion was of dogs. It was possible he hated them and/or was petrified of them. Hopefully he wasn't allergic to them.

Along with all the dog-related supplies Claire purchased for Lucy, she also picked up a book on Shelties. After barely reading it she already found out she'd brought home a dog who was bred to work. That was the last thing on Claire's mind! Also, it was permissible to shave a Sheltie in the summer, so she would make sure to have that done, once Lucy had matured enough to have a long, shaggy coat.

Although Lucy was a ways away from taking a walk, it wasn't too soon for her to learn what the leash was. It wasn't as if she didn't have enough energy and coordination to walk at least a little bit. What little time Claire had so far spent with Lucy, made her realize how lonely she'd been the past two years.

Claire started the leash training in the backyard, and Lucy appeared to be a quick learner. With Drake returning home soon, it was possible the three of them could take a short walk together, even if it was just around the walled backyard. The entire property was close to two acres, and although the two-story house itself took up quite a bit of area, the backyard was still spacious.

After Claire had walked Lucy around the perimeter of the backyard, it was time for a break. Claire needed to put the roast for dinner, in the oven. Drake had long ago made it clear he never wanted to go out to eat the same day he returned from a long business trip.

The roast cooking, Claire checked the time. In another hour her husband would be home. She could hardly wait. The only thing that tempered her was knowing his reception of her would be cordial but not over-the-top. Whenever Claire had a crisis of confidence, she'd remind herself, her husband had never before married, until she came along. Therefore, she was worth something, if only to him!

Although Claire had dutifully purchased a metal "crate" for Lucy, per the saleslady's insistence, Claire was against it all the way. Growing up, her family never used one of those confining cages to housebreak a puppy. Instead, her father would beat the shit out of a dog until it "figured things out." However, since the overpriced metal crate was on Drake's dime, it was no big deal. The bottom line was, although Claire probably should have put Lucy in her crate while dinner was being prepared, Claire failed to do so. In turn, the puppy proceeded to make a mess, but not the kind one would have assumed.

It all had to do with the fact Drake discreetly returned from his trip, in order to surprise Claire. He'd purchased a beautiful bracelet for her while overseas and was suddenly determined to make their life together "more interesting." He was aware the long spaces of time he was away on business trips, were making Claire lonely, but he had no choice. Although it appeared he was his own boss and Claire assumed as much, there were "higher-ups." The last thing Drake could do was reveal his true nature as it were. It would be the end of him, in the literal sense. All this came back around to why he'd never wanted a dog (and owning a cat was even more out of the question): it could potentially blow his cover.

Anyway, Drake had been dropped off at his house by the limo driver he always used and decided to enter the house via the side door leading to the garage. Once inside he could go in the house via "the mud room," which led directly to the kitchen. Usually he came right in the front door, and even if Claire didn't hear him enter, she would immediately see him, despite most likely being in front of the stove or the countertop area nearby, making dinner. Although she was lazy, he could count on her to cook for him, and she was very capable. On this occasion, she was leaning over the sink when Drake snuck up on her, and it appeared she was rinsing a pan. He was so busy staring at the back of her jet black head of hair (supposedly she was a natural blonde but he wouldn't know it), he didn't realize a dog was lying in the very corner he was sneaking around! Therefore, he surprised the hell out of the dog, who in turn surprised Drake by leaping up and grabbing his right hand—but not hard. The problem was Drake overreacted and jerked his arm away, only to lose his whole hand in the process. Once the dog realized what happened, it dropped the hand in nothing flat. It was a good boy (or girl?), all right. Otherwise it would have tried to take off with the fake body part.

By this time Claire had turned around and at first was thrilled to see Drake, exclaiming, "Honey, you're home!" Then she stepped closer, only to see his hand lying on the white ceramic tile floor. She probably wondered why there wasn't any blood. Drake calmly picked up the hand and stuck it back in place. Then, from his navy suit coat pocket he removed a dark green velvet jewelry box, containing a million-dollar, diamond and gold bracelet. Once he gave it to her and explained himself, she'd never question anything. That was important because she was part of a global experiment to integrate robots with civilians. If she hadn't been so shallow and hell-bent on finding an exceptionally good-looking mate, she could have avoided her predicament!

Drake would let Claire keep the dog, provided it accepted him for what he really was. If she had instead suddenly decided they needed to start a family, that would have been an issue. In the meantime, Drake would keep a close eye on the Martins, down the street. Ever since they were briefed on "the real goings on," they seemed to think it wasn't necessary to wave. Maybe he'd tell Claire everyone on the street was a robot, so she'd never acknowledge them when she walked her new dog. That would serve them right. As it was, other than her dog, she was pretty much all alone.

Amy has written several novels and short story collections, including *Retribution and Other Twisted Tales* in 2016, *Dogs and Their Twisted Tales* in 2017, and *More Dogs and Their Twisted Tales—and One Cat Story in 2018.* She resides on a horse farm in Indiana. AmyKristoff.com.

CPSIA information can be obtained
at www.ICGtesting.com
Printed in the USA
FSHW011501250319

9 781937 869090